Friedrich Glauser was born in Vienna in 1896. Often referred to as the Swiss Simenon, he died aged forty-two, a few days before he was due to be married. Diagnosed a schizophrenic, addicted to morphine and opium, he spent much of his life in psychiatric wards, insane asylums and, when he was arrested for forging prescriptions, in prison. He also spent two years with the Foreign Legion in North Africa, after which he worked as a coal miner and a hospital orderly. His Sergeant Studer crime novels have ensured his place as a cult figure in Europe.

Germany's most prestigious crime-fiction award is called the Glauser prize.

Other Bitter Lemon books featuring Sergeant Studer

Thumbprint
In Matto's Realm
Fever
The Chinaman

THE SPOKE

Friedrich Glauser

Translated from the German
by Mike Mitchell

BITTER LEMON PRESS
LONDON

BITTER LEMON PRESS
First published in the United Kingdom in 2008 by
Bitter Lemon Press, 37 Arundel Gardens, London W11 2LW
www.bitterlemonpress.com
Originally published in German as *Krock & Co.*
in the Beobachter, Basel, in 1937

This edition published in German as *Die Speiche*
by Limmat Verlag, Zurich in 1996

Bitter Lemon Press gratefully acknowledges the financial
assistance of Pro Helvetia, the Arts Council of Switzerland

swiss arts council
pr☐helvetia

German-language edition © Limmat Verlag, 1996
English translation © Mike Mitchell, 2008

A CIP record for this book is available from the
British Library

ISBN 978–1–904738–27–5

Typeset by Alma Books Limited
Printed and bound in Great Britain by
Cox & Wyman Ltd, Reading, Berkshire

The Spoke

The Interrupted Wedding

Why had he given in? Why had he let his wife and daughter have their way? Now he was stuck here and might even get his knuckles rapped for having acted without authorization and not left the body in the garden behind the house, where it had been found . . .

* * *

The dead man was lying on the table, white with years of scrubbing, in the cellar of the Hôtel zum Hirschen, a thin trickle of blood winding across the wooden surface. Slowly the drops fell on the cement floor – it sounded like the ticking of a clock weary with age.

The dead man: young, tall, very slim, wearing light grey flannel trousers and a dark blue polo shirt, his long arms covered in blond hair sticking out of the short sleeves.

And beside his head the murder weapon. Not a knife, not a revolver, an unusual murder weapon, one he'd never seen before: the spoke of a bicycle wheel, filed to a point at one end. It hadn't been easy to find, stuck as it was in the dead man's body, the end hardly protruding at all. Studer had only noticed it when he ran his hand over the corpse's back. It had been thrust almost vertically down into the body from just below the left shoulder blade and had not come out anywhere, neither at the chest nor the stomach. They wouldn't know how many vital organs the skewer had pierced until the doctor had performed the autopsy.

Such a small piece of the blunt end of the spoke had been sticking out that he'd had to use a pair of pliers to pull it out.

So the first question was: how had the murderer held the weapon? It must have had some kind of handle when the man was stabbed. Could it have been screwed off? Afterwards? That seemed a possibility, since there was an almost invisible spiral thread cut into the blunt end of the spoke. A real mechanic had been at work, no doubt about that.

Detective Sergeant Studer of the Bern Police would have dearly loved to light up a Brissago, but that wasn't on, not right beside the body. So there was nothing left for it but to pace up and down the narrow room, in the horribly bright light from the bulb dangling from a dusty wire, while he lectured Albert.

But each of his monologues started with a question, in

his broadest Bernese: "Just look at this, Bärtu. Why the hell did we listen to our womenfolk?"

That very day Albert Guhl, a powerfully built, broad-shouldered twenty-nine-year-old corporal in the Thurgau Cantonal Police, stationed in Arbon, had married Studer's daughter.

Couldn't the wedding, the sergeant went on, just as well have been held in Bern? No, they'd insisted it took place in Arbon. "Because your mother's an old woman and isn't keen on travelling? That's a reason, I suppose, but is it reason enough? What d'you think, Bärtu?"

Albert Guhl said nothing. Studer raised his massive shoulders; his hands rose with them, then came down with a smack on his thighs.

"And now?" He went slowly over to the table, bent down and looked at the dead man's face.

An unpleasant face! A long curved nose, like a vulture's beak, two deep furrows running from the nose to the corners of the mouth, the lips pursed, revealing the teeth – and it looked as if the dead man were smiling, with all his gold fillings. The only good thing was that Studer had closed the dead man's eyes – it had been the first thing he'd done once the skewer, the spoke, had been pulled out of his back. That look! Studer remembered it, full of scorn, even in death.

Didn't it look as if the murdered man were mocking those still alive? Hardly had this question occurred to the sergeant than he asked it out loud. And Albert, his son-in-law, nodded – nodded but didn't open his mouth.

"Cat got your tongue?" Studer enquired.

Albert looked up, shook his head and said, mildly, not as a reproach, "We should have left him there, Father."

"Left him there! . . . Left him there!" Irascibly Studer imitated the younger man's tone of voice. "Left him there! So the local peasants could trample all over the ground? Eh? So we wouldn't find any clues? Eh?"

"Clues!" Albert said softly, his voice full of a placatory respect, which mollified the sergeant. "With the ground as it is, I don't think we'll find many clues, Father . . ."

"Because it's dry as a bug's backside? Eh? Is that what you're saying, young lad? Then I think you should know that Sergeant Studer" – he was so worked up he really did talk of himself in the third person – "managed to solve a similar case. The body was on ground that was just as dry – in a forest!" But Studer's irritation had blown over by now, he was just putting it on. Albert was well aware of that, and smiled. "Yes! In a forest, the ground covered in pine needles," Studer repeated, thrusting his fists so deep into his pockets that the sound of cloth tearing could be clearly heard in the sudden silence.

10

"Dammit!" the sergeant muttered. "Now my wallet's going to fall out. And why, oh why," he sighed, "did we have to come to Schwarzenstein, for God's sake?"

"But Father," Albert said, "you suggested the Hôtel zum Hirschen in Schwarzenstein yourself."

Studer grunted. That was true, unfortunately. He had suggested the hotel. Over lunch in Arbon someone had mentioned the old wedding-day custom of driving out in carriages to some little village in the Appenzell countryside, and it had occurred to the sergeant that a childhood sweetheart of his ran a hotel in Schwarzenstein. First love never dies, they say, so it wasn't two women (Studer's wife and daughter) who were to blame for the unfortunate end to the outing, but three. Anni Ibach, now Frau Anna Rechsteiner, who – forty years ago? . . . thirty-eight? – anyway, a long time ago had been to school in an Emmenthal village with Köbu Studer, had to take her share.

Poor Anni! She hadn't exactly hit the jackpot when she'd married Karl Rechsteiner in St Gallen ten years ago. They'd bought the hotel in Schwarzenstein. At first all had gone well, lots of holidaymakers went to stay there in the summer, but then her husband had fallen ill. He'd been bedridden for three years now, and once he'd had to go to a sanatorium in the South Tyrol.

"Consumption," said Dr Salvisberg, who was treating him.

And Rechsteiner certainly did not look well, not at all well. Anni had taken Studer to see him that afternoon and since then he couldn't get the sight out of his mind. Above all the man's face: smooth, pinched, the left side smaller than the right; and his skin – the colour of clay.

No, things were not easy for Anni. She was on her feet all day: she had to keep an eye on the staff, the stable – four cows, two horses, several goats – and the fields. Then the hotel: the kitchen, the cutlery and crockery, the laundry. At the same time she had to be nice to the holidaymakers, so that they came back the next year. They brought in the money – and Rechsteiner needed a lot! The doctor, medicines, the sanatorium.

And now this murder. It might keep the visitors away. Who wants to stay in a hotel where a murder's been committed? And such a mysterious one? It would be in the newspapers, the serious ones perhaps less than the tabloids; a sensational crime like this was a godsend for them. So Anni had asked the sergeant to help her. Could a man refuse such a request? Especially when it came from your childhood sweetheart. And then Anni. She'd shown how brave she could be as a girl, at school. And she was still as plucky as ever. Not a single complaint had crossed her lips, not even when the body had been found in the garden behind the hotel, just a shy request, no, not even that, a statement rather: Köbu'll sort it all out.

Once more Studer was by the table, looking at the dead man. Beside the head was the spoke from a bicycle wheel that had been filed to a sharp point. With a shake of his head he picked up the strange weapon, held it under the light bulb and gave it a thorough examination.

And suddenly he made his first discovery.

"Bärtu," he called out softly. When his son-in-law came over to him Studer was holding a stiff grey hair between his thumb and forefinger. "Have a look at that."

"Hm," said Albert.

And what did he mean by "Hm", Studer wanted to know. Had all the Thurgauers had their lips sewn up? "What kind of a hair is that?"

"Not a human hair," Albert said cautiously.

The sergeant gave a snort of contempt. A two-year-old baby could tell it wasn't a human hair. But what kind of animal was it from? A goat? A lamb? A rabbit? A horse? A cow?

The hair the sergeant was still holding between his thumb and forefinger was thin, stiff and shiny. As long as his finger.

Shyly Albert voiced the opinion that it looked as if it

might be a dog's hair, at which he was informed that policemen didn't just guess, they had to prove things. What had made him think it might be a dog's hair?

"Because when we all arrived there was a long-haired dog jumping up at the horses. It was exactly that colour – and the length of its hair was the same too."

Studer nodded and patted his son-in-law on the shoulder; they might make something of him yet. Then he went to the door and flung it open. Albert heard steps going up some stairs.

About five minutes later the sergeant was back, pushing a midget of a man along in front of him. The little man had a bulbous red nose, so heavy it seemed to pull his head forward.

"Take a seat," said Studer, placing a chair in the middle of the room in such a way that anyone sitting on it couldn't see the dead body.

And once again Sergeant Studer of the Bern Police prepared to play the game which he maintained, in moments of weakness, corrupted people. But by now it had become so much second nature to him that it was perhaps the reason why he had rejected the offer of early retirement. It gave him power over other people and he knew the rules better than many an examining magistrate; he even preferred it to the billiards he played during his free time.

The game began with the usual questions.

"Name?" – "Küng. Johannes Küng."

"Age?" – "Fifty-nine."

"Profession?" – "Groom."

"So you were the one who found the body?" – "Yes."

"Where?" – "In the garden be'ind the 'otel."

"At what time?"

The little man was silent. He rubbed his huge nose with a black forefinger. Then he stopped doing that and, with great difficulty – his green apron was in the way – took a huge silver pocket watch out of his waistcoat pocket. He stared at it for a long time, then said in a quiet voice, "A quarter to ten." The watch returned to its pocket behind the green apron.

"You're sure?" Studer asked.

"As God's my witness."

Why then wasn't the landlady informed until a quarter past ten?

First of all, Küng explained, he'd had to give the horses their oats, since the guests wanted to leave at half past ten.

"So you just left the dead man there in the garden?"

A nod; a long, silent nod.

"OK. And you recognized the man?"

Again the silent nod of the head that was beginning to try the sergeant's patience.

"Well, come on, tell me, Küng," he said, irritated, "who was it?"

"'Is name's Stieger. 'E came to visit someone. On Sunday. Worked in St Gallen – An' the woman too. I think" – Küng scratched his nose – "I think they both work in the same office."

"The woman?" Studer asked. "Which woman?"

"Loppacher. Martha Loppacher. She's on 'oliday, conver . . . convalescin' – 'cause she's been ill. She's been 'ere four weeks."

Silence. Studer had taken out his notebook and written down the names in his tiny writing that looked as if it were made up of Greek letters.

Stieger, he wrote, putting a cross behind the name, and *Loppacher, Martha*. Then it suddenly struck him that everything so far had indeed been nothing but a game, since he already knew everything he'd been asking about. But there'd been so much else as well – the confusion, the women screaming, bringing the body in – that the sergeant felt the need to bring some order to his thoughts.

"Four weeks?" he asked, pondering. "And what's she been doing all this time?"

"Er . . . goin' for walks, readin' . . . sleepin' in the meadows . . . An' cuddlin' . . ."

Studer glanced at his son-in-law, but he didn't seem to have noticed, so the sergeant had to keep his amusement at Küng's expression to himself and his smile hidden behind his moustache.

"Cuddling?" he repeated. "How do you mean?"

"Goin' round with men."

"Who with? All of them, or just one?"

"'Speshly with Ernstli – Ernst Graf. A reg'lar buck, is Ernstli."

"Ernst Graf? And what does he do?"

"Bicycles."

"What, bicycles? He sells them? Repairs them?"

"Yes."

"And does this Ernst Graf have a dog?"

"Course 'e does."

"What kind of dog?"

"You gen'lmen must've seen it. Jumpin' up all round the 'orses' legs when you arrived, it were."

Studer could see the dog clearly in his mind's eye. A kind of Pomeranian, a mongrel really, with a grey coat and thick, bristly hair.

Ernst Graf had a bicycle shop? The murder weapon was the spoke from a bicycle wheel! And he had a dog as well? . . . Just a minute. A dog hair and a spoke didn't constitute proof. No, it needed more than that. Above all, he needed to get to know this Ernst Graf. How had Küng put it? The man was a . . . yes, that was it, "a reg'lar buck". What that suggested to Studer was the village stud, a handsome lad, none too bright but good at sweet-talking the women. He was all the more surprised, then, to learn that Graf was over fifty.

"Over fifty?" he repeated in astonishment. "Isn't that a little old for a 'reg'lar buck'?"

At that the midget with the bulbous nose burst out laughing. He laughed and laughed, which made Studer furious because he realized he was being made fun of. That was what you got when a detective from Bern poked his nose into a case in another canton. But, God knows, he was only doing it to help Anni Ibach, his childhood sweetheart. It was only after she had asked him that he'd promised to look into the case.

"So that it'll be over and done with sooner," Anni had said. "Otherwise it'll keep the visitors away, and they'll be putting the place up for auction by the winter!"

This Küng was the first real obstacle. Wouldn't it be more sensible to get his son-in-law to take over here? He came from the area and knew the customs better – and the language! No. He had to show his son-in-law that he wasn't ripe for the scrapheap yet, that the Bernese weren't the buffoons people in the east of Switzerland took them for.

18

The heat in the cellar was simply unbearable. Flies were buzzing round the light bulb, settling on the dead man's face, running up and down his bare arms, arms that were long and thin, pale too, like most city folk's.

Suddenly Studer had tired of his game. Because it had suddenly turned serious, or because it was long past midnight? He couldn't have said why, but he was fed up with it and that was that. In the morning the examining magistrate would be coming with his clerk and the chief of Appenzell Canton Police. Let those gentlemen deal with the case. The only nuisance was that no one was allowed to leave the hotel, so the wedding party would have to spend the night there. It was turning out to be an expensive excursion! Three coachmen, six horses – thank God the wedding party wasn't a large one: Albert's mother, two uncles, three aunts; the only ones from Bern were Studer and his wife. He decided he would share the expenses of the outing with Albert's mother.

After one more quick look at the dead man he ushered Albert and Küng out of the cellar and switched off the light. He didn't close the door; first of all he went to ask Anni for a sheet for the corpse. Then he went back to the cellar and spread it over the body. He spent a long time holding the end and staring at the dead man's features.

"Nasty," he whispered. "Nasty, that's the word." Finally he covered up the man's face.

Then he switched off the light, locked the door and went up to their room. His wife was already in bed. He went onto the balcony, lit a Brissago and looked out over the quiet countryside.

The road was a long white ribbon disappearing into the darkness to the right and left. The hillside across the valley was fairly steep and from below the soft babbling of a stream could be heard. The June night smelled of new-mown hay, flowers, a scattering of manure. Another smell made its presence felt. At first Studer didn't recognize it, then he suddenly realized what it was: there was a clear smell of old, rusty iron that had been warmed by the sun during the day and was now giving off the stored heat. The sergeant leaned over the railing and saw a dilapidated old shed to the right of the hotel, by the edge of the road. And then a veil of cloud suddenly split and the moon, no bigger than a slice of lemon, flooded the countryside with its light, revealing the piles of junk all round the shed: old wheels, rusty barrel hoops . . . On the side of the shed a white sign with black writing gleamed:

"Ernst Graf – Bicycles."

Aha! So the "reg'lar buck" lived right next to the inn – sorry, to the Hôtel zum Hirschen.

A sleepy voice from inside the room expressed the opinion that it was about time Father came to bed. Tomorrow was another day, it added. With a sigh Detective Sergeant Studer of the Bern Police threw away his half-smoked cigar, which scattered a few sparks as it hit the road, like some dud firework. He went back into the room and undressed in the dark. The bedsprings creaked and the sleepy voice asked whether Köbu had found anything?

"No!" Studer growled angrily. Then: "Off to sleep now, Hedy."

A sigh, followed by a truly female remark: "I only hope this murder doesn't bring the children bad luck," Hedy said.

Chabis – rubbish – was Studer's response. He was a little superstitious himself but kept it secret. Then he lay back, his hands clasped behind his head, staring into the darkness. The moon pursued its course. Now it was shining into the room and the sergeant, staring at it, his eyes wide open, had the feeling it resembled someone. Both in its shape and its colour. He racked his brains . . . and suddenly he had it: Rechsteiner, the husband of his childhood sweetheart, the landlord of the Hôtel zum Hirschen, had a lopsided face, just like the waning moon. His skin was yellow, like the moon. In his mind's eye Studer could see the sick man's face, very clear and sharp, as it had rested on the pillows that afternoon.

Ernst Graf and "Fräulein" Loppacher

Studer woke at half past three. It was already light outside. He got out of bed quietly, so as not to wake his wife, picked up his black boots and crept out, across the corridor and down the stairs. He stood by the door to the cellar for a while, listening . . . The rest of the hotel was quiet, as quiet as the room behind the door. Softly Studer opened it, went in and crossed the room to the table. He had no idea what he was doing there. Then he remembered that they hadn't searched the man's clothes the previous evening.

He threw back the sheet. Going through the pockets wouldn't be difficult, there were only his trousers: a wallet . . . Four twenties, three fives, coins . . . a handkerchief . . . a pocket knife on a chain . . . in the back pocket a wallet so well filled it had stretched the cloth.

Letters, letters, letters:

Herr Jean Stieger, 25 Bahnhofstrasse, St Gallen.

Hmm. Herr Stieger couldn't call himself Johann or Hans like any normal man from St Gallen. Jean! Presumably he'd thought it more refined. Well, that was his affair.

The same handwriting on all the envelopes: large letters,

sloping to the left with club-like growths on the horizontal strokes. Twenty envelopes – and all of them empty.

Not one single letter! Studer shook his head, baffled. What was the point of carrying empty envelopes round with you? He had a closer look at the stamps; they had a Schwarzenstein postmark. He laid them all out on a corner of the table and established that the first had been sent on 12 May, the last on 20 June. Twenty letters in thirty-nine days: a letter every two days on average. Nor was the sender's name difficult to establish; clearly written on the back of the envelopes was "Fräulein Martha Loppacher, Hôtel zum Hirschen, Schwarzenstein". Studer shook his head. That Martha Loppacher must think no end of herself – to insist on calling yourself "Fräulein" on the back of an envelope!

But what had happened to the letters, which surely had still been in the envelopes the previous day? Studer stared into space. In his mind's eye he could still see the scene in the little garden behind the hotel: the sparse light of two torches, one held by the groom, Küng, one by his son-in-law Albert, shining on the dead man, lying on his belly and . . . Studer put his thumb and forefinger over his eyes to help him visualize the body – yes, now he could see it! The button of the back pocket had definitely – definitely – been fastened. There was a flap over the top, with a buttonhole and the dark shimmer of a button holding the flap down.

That was yesterday evening, at a quarter past ten. Then Studer had called his son-in-law and they'd carried the body into the cellar. Why into the cellar? Anni Rechsteiner had led the way. After that Studer had kept watch with Albert, interrogated Küng, gone to fetch a sheet and then locked the door . . .

And now the pocket was unbuttoned and the twenty envelopes empty.

That the key to the cellar had been in Studer's pocket all night meant nothing – there would be several keys to the door. But that left one question: what was the point of removing the letters and leaving the empty envelopes? Wouldn't it have been simpler to take both at once? The sergeant replaced the wallet and stowed the envelopes in the inside pocket of his black jacket. He remembered he'd brought his camera. That was something he could do that evening, something to look forward to. But he needed various things: two boxes of plates, a printing frame, developer, fixative, intensifier . . .

Studer made sure the cellar door was properly locked, then slipped silently along the corridors of the hotel cellars on his stockinged feet until he found a back door that was open. He squatted down, put on his boots and went out into the morning air, full of loud birdsong. He'd only taken six steps, and his boots were already wet. There was a heavy dew on the short grass.

Below the sign "Ernst Graf – Bicycles" was a door painted red. It was an unpleasant red, recalling congealed blood. There was a vertical handle screwed onto the door with a latch above it. Studer grasped the handle and pressed down the latch with his thumb. The door wasn't locked and swung open.

The yard inside reflected the state of the ground outside the building: old iron everywhere, barrel hoops, chains, sheets of metal, rusty iron pans. Somewhere a pig grunted, goats bleated, a sheep baaed. But this peaceful concert was drowned out by loud barking that started with a furious crescendo then grew quieter, as if the animal had gone hoarse or was being throttled by a collar. Across from the gate was a single-storey house, not really a house, a shack rather, with a lower shed built up against it, from which the animals' morning chorus and the hoarse barking came. Studer went over to the house, knocked briefly and pushed at the door. It too was open.

But he didn't go straight in. You could have cut the air that came streaming out with a knife: tobacco, sweat, animals.

"Hey! Graf! You up yet?"

Silence. Studer listened and felt a faint flutter of fear, as if there was something wrong here too. But then it was calmed by the deep, regular snoring. The bicycle dealer must be sleeping soundly, and if that was the sleep of the just, then Ernst Graf had nothing to do with the murder. A gentle morning breeze brushed over Studer's back, slipped into the room, danced around a little then swirled out again. The sergeant was grateful to it for sweeping out the fetid air.

A grimy table in the middle of the room, a bare light bulb above it hanging from a black wire. The cupboard in the corner was askew. The only decoration was a calendar on the wall with a picture surrounded by the months. Impossible to see what the picture was, though – all those flies! Cobwebs in the corners, round the light, on the wire. A rusty stove with a spirit-burner on it . . . But where was the man?

He closed the door. Behind it he discovered a pile of grubby blankets emitting snores. He went across and bent down – the man had pulled the bedclothes over his head. The sergeant shook him. The snoring stopped. Studer shook him again, more vigorously. The blankets were flung aside, but what he saw was not the man, but a tiny piglet, pink and clean, which stared up at him, blinked in the light and gave out a high, piercing squeal. Only then did Studer see the man.

His face was dark, almost black, the result of stubble as well as grime. He hadn't undressed, he was wearing blue mechanic's overalls, the top part open revealing a shirt that had once, but a long time ago, also been blue.

"Wha—?" the man grunted, rubbing his eyes with his clenched fists. "Wha—?" he repeated, looking round the kitchen. Then he called out in a croaky voice, "Ideli!" and the piglet trotted over, as obedient to its name as a dog, and sat down on the blankets with a contented sigh. And the man stroked the animal, assuring it that it was a good little piglet. The sergeant stood observing this example of animal training with arms akimbo, elbows sticking out. He was close to letting his jaw drop with amazement. As it was, his mouth was open and it was only thanks to his moustache that it wasn't obvious.

Graf behaved as if he were alone in the room. He got up and gave himself a good scratch. His hair was black, with a bluish tinge, and grew so low down on his forehead it almost reached his eyebrows. The stubble covered his cheeks right up to his nose and stuck out from his chin.

Graf shuffled round the room, barefoot, apparently looking for something. The strange thing was that his feet were white and clean – just the soles gradually got darker as they picked up dirt from the floor. Studer was willing to bet he'd washed them the previous evening. Why his feet? Why not his face?

He continued to shuffle round, opened the cupboard and looked inside – and inside it was tidy, with clean under-wear piled up neatly on the shelves. Finally he found what he was looking for. He had a tiny, round pocket mirror in his right hand and was subjecting himself to a close inspection. And pulling faces into the bargain!

Still treating the sergeant as if he wasn't there, he trotted over to the door and went out. The animal chorus swelled and Studer witnessed a remarkable scene.

The sheep came up and rubbed its muzzle against the man's trouser-leg. "*Salut*, Mousie," Graf said, enquiring if it had slept well. There followed two goats, snow-white, with no horns but white lappets hanging down on each side of their heads. "Hi, kids," the man said and asked if they were hungry. The two goats seemed to understand since they nodded wisely and trotted off, followed by the sheep, to a hole in the fence where they set about nibbling the grass coming up among the scrap iron. "And Bruin too," said the man, untying the dog, which was jumping up and down. But the language he used to communicate with the dog was so bizarre the sergeant could not understand a word.

Studer felt he looked ridiculous, standing there in the

middle of the little farmyard in his best black suit. It didn't go with the sun, which was already getting pretty warm, or with the scrap iron; it didn't go with Ernst Graf and his animals. His black Sunday suit was like a suit of armour, cutting him off from the outside world, from the trees and the grass, from the animals and the barefoot man.

The latter pumped some water into a basin and started playing at being a seal, putting his head in, pulling it out, snorting, shaking the water off. Then he took off his overall and shirt and pumped water over his back. The dog jumped up around him, barking, until the basin of water was poured over its head and it shook, snorted and sneezed as its master had done. The piglet was lying on the doorstep, legs stretched out, blinking in the sun.

"Ideli!" the man shouted. When the piglet showed no sign of moving, he went over to pick it up and washed it under the pump with an old brush.

Just as Studer was about to announce his presence – he was beginning to get impatient; he wasn't used to being ignored – the man asked whether the sergeant would like a cup of coffee. It gave Studer a start. How did Graf know who he was, he asked. He'd actually been expecting the sergeant all night, the man explained, but he'd got fed up by two o'clock and had gone to bed. However, they had plenty of time for a chat now.

"Come in," said the man, using the familiar *du* as if it were the most natural thing in the world.

The sergeant had no problem with the familiar form of address, it was standard in the Bernese countryside, but drink coffee in that shack? On that grubby table? Perhaps even out of unwashed mugs? Studer felt like declining out of consideration for his Sunday suit – and for his stomach. He was just about to say no when the latch on the gate to the yard went up with a loud click, the door opened and . . .

In the doorway stood "Fräulein" Martha Loppacher – in his mind Studer did indeed place the "Fräulein" in inverted commas. The previous evening she had put on a rather hysterical performance, wringing her hands, sobbing and crying out. She had thrown herself down beside the body and kept on crying, "My beloved! My beloved!" until it was too much for everyone and Frau Studer had decided to take the "Fräulein" back into the hotel by force. What happened to her after that Studer didn't know. He had forgotten Martha Loppacher.

Now she was standing in the gateway to the yard in a sleeveless frock that was pretty short. Her fingernails were painted red, her eyebrows shaved and drawn in with pencil, her lips as red as her fingernails. The gentle morning breeze, which had kindly aired the stinking room and continued its useful activity, took flight, clearly frightened off by the thick layer of powder covering Fräulein Loppacher's cheeks.

Tears? Sadness? Not a bit! Fräulein Loppacher came in with a smile on her face and speaking the formal German she clearly thought more refined than her native Swiss.

"Good morning, Herr Studer, you already up as well? How is your dear wife? She was so kind to me yesterday night in my sorrow, like a mother, I truly am eternally grateful to her – Good morning, Herr Graf." She held out a gracious hand to the black-faced man (the washing had not made a great deal of difference).

Graf took the four proffered fingers in his great paw and squeezed them until the Fräulein gave a high-pitched shriek.

"Ouch! Leggo, you randy goat!"

Studer nodded. He got the picture. And when the offer of coffee was repeated, he accepted without demur. Graf led the way but didn't show his guests into his bedroom. He opened a door to the right of it; the room inside was rather different.

A workshop, very clean. Below the wide window a table, the top three inches thick. Vices attached to it and, nailed to the wall beside the window, strips of leather holding tools: adjustable spanners, screwdrivers, files. Bicycle frames wrapped in brown paper were hanging from the ceiling, and in one corner there was a small portable forge. Graf raked the ashes, stepped on the bellows and threw some coal on the meagre flame. Then he went to the pump to fill a pan with water and put it on the fire. He worked the bellows again and, when the water started to simmer, took a bag of coffee beans from an unpainted wall-cupboard.

Then a tablecloth appeared on the further end of the workbench with three cups on it, a coffee pot, bread, butter, honey.

Ernst Graf had put on a clean shirt.

One thing was clear: the bicycle dealer and the office worker were in love.

It didn't take particularly keen powers of observation to see that. Glances, inflections, the first names, the familiar *du* that kept on slipping out. Studer grinned to himself, but at the same time he felt a tug at his heartstrings. Heaven knows why, but he felt genuine affection for the "reg'lar buck". Was it the love the man showed towards his animals or his gruff but at the same time friendly manner? Studer shook his head imperceptibly as he stroked Bruin gently and then looked at the hairs left on his hand. No doubt about it, the hair sticking to the murder weapon had come from this dog. Poor beast! Its master was presumably going to spend the next night in prison in Trogen. You didn't need to be a great prophet to predict that. Just let the examining magistrate and the chief of Appenzell police get their hands on the case! They'd accuse the man straight away.

Graf sold and repaired bicycles – and the murder weapon was a spoke that had been filed to a sharp point. The dog hair. And they only had to listen to the village gossip to find their motive, handed to them on a plate: jealousy.

Studer felt he was powerless, here, away from his own canton. Assuming he attempted to convince the examining magistrate of Graf's innocence, what would be the result? He could already hear the loud guffaws. What! A simple detective, a cop from outside – and from Bern at that – trying to teach the magistrate, a university graduate, his job? Hahahaha! Get off home, they'd tell him, and don't poke your nose into affairs that aren't your business. Who in the half-canton of Appenzell AusserRhoden had any idea that in a previous existence Sergeant Studer had been a chief inspector with the Bern city police? That he had worked with Gross in Graz, Reiss in Lausanne and Locard in Lyons? That he was the one they usually sent as a delegate to police conferences?

That was no use here. He'd have to go about things

differently. In the first place he'd have to stay in the background. And then he'd have to get to know everyone involved, gradually gain their confidence, live with them for a while, putting together his little observations, everyday things, like laying the hardcore bed for a road, patiently, one stone after another until finally the road's finished – and it leads to the guilty man.

But all that would take time, a lot of time.

Why not, thought Studer. He'd taken a week's holiday for his daughter's wedding and he was happy to make use of the time. The air out there was healthy, certainly healthier than in Thunstrasse in Bern, where the Studers had their apartment. The only question was whether he should stay by himself in Schwarzenstein or keep his wife and the newlyweds there too. No, he thought, his family would just get in the way. But he needed Albert. There'd be tears, he could see that; in such matters women could not be brought to see reason. But Studer hadn't been married for twenty-five years without learning how to get his own way, despite moans and tears. You just had to stick your hands in your pockets, hunch your shoulders and keep your head down until the rain stopped.

No, he wanted to keep Albert there with him. Studer had a funny feeling – like the feeling you get before a storm when the air's heavy and there are just a few clouds visible on the horizon – he felt that the murder of this Jean Stieger was only the beginning. A prelude, so to speak. What would come next? Well, first of all the police and the examining magistrate would appear and arrest the bicycle dealer on a tried and trusted principle: first catch your guilty person and the proof will turn up automatically. And then? But what was the point of worrying about things that hadn't happened yet?

Did he know, the sergeant asked Graf, that the murder weapon was a bicycle spoke filed to a sharp point?

Graf nodded. He'd been there when the body was discovered.

"Is that so?"

"As God's my witness, yes, definitely."

"Where were you?"

"Oh, I kept in the background. I didn't want the landlady to see me."

"The landlady?"

"Yes, Anni Rechsteiner. She gets angry if she sees me near the inn."

"Why?"

"Well, both of them, her and her husband, say the mess and the scrap iron drive away the customers."

"And is that true?"

"No, quite the opposite. The visitors like to come and chat with me in my workshop. I know all the best Appenzell jokes."

"Why did you send letters to the late Herr Stieger every other day, Fräulein Loppacher?" Studer suddenly asked. As he did so he was looking not at the woman but at Graf, who pulled a face, as if he had toothache, and opened his mouth, as if he were going to say something. His clenched fists were on the table, motionless, but his forearms were quivering slightly.

"Every other day?" Fräulein Loppacher said in her "refined" tones. "You're exaggerating, Herr Studer. True, I did write to him quite often, but mostly just on business matters. We worked in the same office and since Herr Stieger had taken over part of my responsibilities during my absence, I needed to tell him about various things . . . various things . . ." she repeated, drumming on the table with her painted fingernails.

"This office," said Studer, "it's in St Gallen, isn't it? Yes? And what kind of business does it do?"

"It deals with . . ." her reply was hesitant, "it deals with legal questions . . . Advice on commercial matters, on involved civil actions, drawing up wills and deeds of gift. As well as that, in particularly complicated cases we have also undertaken inquiries, searched for missing persons.

And there is a department attached which provides . . . information . . ."

"Information?"

"Yes. A kind of private detective agency."

"And who owns the firm?"

"Joachim Krock. But Herr Stieger was a partner. He had invested money in the business and was the head of the detective agency. That's where we worked together."

"You were engaged?"

"Certainly not! What put that idea into your head? Never!"

Graf heaved a deep sigh of relief. It sounded like the bellows of his forge letting out air.

"And Herr Stieger came to see you on business yesterday?"

"Yeees . . . er . . . yes." The answer did not sound entirely convincing, but he had to make do with it for the moment, for it was immediately followed by a question. "How did you know I had such frequent correspondence with him, Herr Studer?"

"Because I found your letters on him."

"My letters? That's not possible. I'm sure they're in St Gallen."

"So what's this?" Studer asked, taking the packet of envelopes out of his inside pocket.

There ought to be a law, the sergeant said to himself, against women painting and powdering themselves. The layer covering their cheeks could easily, all too easily, hide a flush, a sudden pallor. He really could not tell what impression the production of the envelopes had made on Fräulein Loppacher, for as well as that, she had half-closed her eyelids and the rest of her eyes were concealed behind the lashes, which were long and, of course, covered in mascara.

"May I see them?" she asked, stretching out her hand, which was trembling slightly.

"I'm sorry," said Studer, "but I have to hand them over to the local police – Hey!" His exclamation was too late. Graf had caught hold of the sergeant's wrist; a quick twist and he was handing the packet to his friend. Martha Loppacher leafed through the envelopes and shrugged her shoulders. "But they're empty," she said, giving them back to Studer.

The sergeant was not even angry. "Right, then, Ernstli," he said to himself, "for that you're going to spend a few days in clink." Without a word he put the envelopes back in his pocket.

There wasn't much more he could learn in the bicycle shop. And after all, he thought, he hadn't gone there in order to play gooseberry for a pair of lovers. Though it might be very informative given the way the woman had cried "My beloved!" the previous evening and thrown herself down beside the dead body. Just like in a film! And that despite the fact that for several weeks now the late Jean Stieger had presumably no longer taken first place in the affections of the heavily made-up Fräulein, who, according to Johannes Küng, was always going round with men. So why the theatrical performance yesterday evening? Who had the young miss been trying to fool?

Ernst Graf had the piglet on his knees, just like a baby, and was feeding it out of a bottle. So that the reason for his departure was not obvious, the sergeant asked another question.

"Did you buy the piglet?"

The answer surprised him. Graf explained that all the animals he had in his stall had been given him. He'd got them from the farmers round about when they were very small and half-dead; but he'd nursed them back to health. He'd taken them to bed with him . . .

"Truly a Saint Anthony," the painted lady declared. Studer gave her a sour look and told her not to mix up her saints. As far as he was aware, it was Saint Francis who had loved animals.

Silence. The piglet heaved a deep sigh, like a satisfied infant. Graf pushed it onto the floor, but it stayed beside him and stood up on its hind legs, placing its front trotters on the man's thighs.

"Bye," said the sergeant. The dog accompanied him to the gate, silent, almost sad, as if it sensed its master was in danger. Studer stroked its head, saying, "Yes, yes, Bruin," but the dog could only give its bushy tail a weary wag.

As the sergeant was crossing the little field separating the hotel from Graf's house, he noticed two things:

Parked by the roadside was a low-slung, red sports car; and the sound of a piano was coming from the open window of the dining room.

He took out his watch. It was six o'clock.

Joachim Krock's Information Bureau

The waitress was wiping the stone steps leading up to the hotel entrance with a damp cloth. Studer asked if his wife was already up – A shake of the head, a silent shake of the head. And the others in the wedding party? – Another shake of the head. But a new guest had arrived? – A nod.

Just like his son-in-law. Just like Küng, the groom. Had the waitress lost her tongue? Impatiently the sergeant asked who the early arrival was.

"From St Gallen . . . a friend of the dead man," the waitress said and splashed his trousers with her wet cloth. His new suit! – Couldn't she be a bit more careful, he snapped – Silence. Studer couldn't repress a smile. He asked – in Italian – why the young lady (*"perché la signorina"*) was annoyed with him.

And then things were fine, as they always are when you treat people in the right way. The waitress, black-haired and solidly built, straightened up, blushed and asked him how he knew she was Italian – From her accent, of course. A conversation developed. She was called Ottilia

Buffatto but here they called her Otti, Studer was told, and she was sorry, oh so sorry that she'd . . . She didn't finish; instead she hurried off and came back with a clean cloth and a basin of water and started to sponge down the sergeant's trousers. While she was doing so the conversation continued.

Oh yes, the landlady! She was so brave ("*una donna valorosa*") despite all her misfortune. Hard at it from morning till night. She kept an eye on everything, the stall with the three cows, the farmhands, the kitchen, the hotel . . . And she still found time to look after the guests. Now, for example, she was already in the dining room talking to the guest who'd arrived early – The piano player? – "*Già!*" Of course! – And who was it playing the piano? The waitress was very sorry but she didn't know. The gentleman had never been there before. But he must be a real gentleman. "*È profumato,*" Otti said; he was wearing perfume – But how did Signora Otti know he came from St Gallen and was a friend of the dead man? – The waitress pointed to the car. It had a St Gallen registration. And, she added, his first question had been about the dead man.

His trousers were clean again. "*Grazie,*" Studer said.

The piano in the dining room fell silent. But only briefly. Then a funeral march floated out on the spring air.

42

Presumably the early arrival was playing it for the dead man lying in the cellar waiting for the authorities to turn up.

The tension in the empty dining room was almost tangible. Anni Ibach (Studer could not bring himself to call his childhood sweetheart "Rechsteiner") was standing beside the piano player and going on at him. In fact, it rather looked as if the man was only playing the piano to make it impossible for anyone to overhear the conversation.

No doubt about it, the two were arguing. They were arguing in low voices and the landlady of the Hôtel zum Hirschen had her fists clenched. She was waving them round in the air and sometimes her right hand came dangerously near to the nose of the man who was sitting, hunched up, on the piano stool. Eavesdrop? Impossible. Studer attempted to creep up on them quietly. In vain! He had the whole of the length of the dining room to cross and not only the parquet floor creaked, his boots did as well. At the very first creak Anni swung round and gave the pianist a nudge with her fist. The funeral march broke off, the piano stool revolved and the man stood up slowly.

A pale-cream silk handkerchief fluttered from the breast pocket of his light blue-grey jacket and a diamond the size of a pea glittered on the little finger of his right hand.

A sloping forehead with sparse black hair, a smooth face with thick lips above a double chin – and his shirt and tie were the same pale cream as his handkerchief. The word "*profumato*" went through the sergeant's mind. The man smelled like a barber's shop: eau de Cologne, brilliantine, toothpaste . . .

"Krock." – "Studer." – "Pleased to meet you." – "Likewise."

It sounded like a declaration of war, and perhaps it was. Herr Krock had thick eyelids and used them to conceal his eyes.

"You're the policeman who took the first details?"

Instead of answering the question, Studer asked for his breakfast. "Anni," he said, "I'd like a cup of coffee."

Anni nodded majestically. "Otti!" she shouted. The waitress appeared in the doorway and the landlady passed on the order.

So she didn't want to leave him alone with the stranger . . . Right, then. So be it. The sergeant accepted the challenge.

"So you've come from St Gallen this early specially to help me solve the murder, have you, Herr Krock?" he asked, sitting uninvited at a table beside the piano, clasping his hands beside his plate. He could see that the edges of his cuffs were dirty and that irritated him. And they were starched cuffs too, not like the other man with his soft, raw-silk shirt.

"I had a telephone call yesterday to say that an accident had happened." Herr Joachim Krock sat down opposite the sergeant. He spoke pure formal German. Anni leaned on the piano.

"From?" Studer asked.

"A young lady who works for me, if you're interested. At midnight."

"You have efficient employees."

"Yes."

Silence. A wasp settled on the rim of the jam bowl. Herr Krock drove it off with an irritated flap of his serviette. Then he cleared his throat. "Don't you think you're taking too much on yourself?" he said. "You're outside your own canton. The authorities here will not approve of your acting independently."

Herr Krock spoke through his nose. He sat there, shoulders hunched, fists on the table, either side of his plate.

"If that's the case, I'll just have to grin and bear it," Studer said impassively, speaking formal German himself. "Did you come all the way from St Gallen just to tell me that?"

"No. I was just looking for some letters my secretary took with him."

"These here?" Studer asked, taking out the envelopes he had found on the dead man. He placed them on the table, an innocent expression on his face.

"Allow me," said Krock, reaching out to pick them up. But he wasn't quick enough. A woman's hand shot between the men's faces down onto the table and scooped up the envelopes.

"They're empty," said the landlady, disappointed.

"Empty?" Krock repeated. Studer nodded. They'd been like that when he'd found them, he said and if Anni would be so good as to give them b—

They fell right in the butter. Studer picked them up, his expression unchanging. Only the bottom envelope had a greasy mark. No harm done. "Anni!" he said.

Why was she interested in the letters one of her guests had written to a man she didn't know?

"Have you seen Martha Loppacher anywhere?" Krock asked. "Her room's empty and Frau Rechsteiner told me Fräulein Loppacher is an early riser."

"Oh yes?" said Studer, his mouth full. The rolls were good, he added, nice and fresh. Oh, and there was the coffee coming already.

Had the sergeant already formed an opinion about the case? Krock wanted to know – An opinion? Studer took a sip of coffee, gave his moustache a good wipe, then said he never had opinions. He was waiting until he'd familiarized himself with the situation there. Then the case would solve itself.

At that Krock got worked up. What? Herr Studer wanted to "familiarize himself" when the facts of the case were completely clear. When it was obvious that the murderer was none other than the jealous bicycle repairer. It was ridiculous, absolutely ridiculous . . . He wiped his brow with his silk handkerchief.

Studer apologized. He'd quite forgotten that Herr Krock was a kind of colleague. Herr Krock was an investigator, a detective, wasn't he? He would be delighted to work together with a man whose criminological skills would be far superior to his own . . .

Having said that, the sergeant took a bite of his roll as the jam was already running down his fingers. When he looked up again he saw an unpleasantly threatening expression in the eyes of the man opposite. But that didn't bother him in the least and he turned to Anni and asked how her husband was. He hoped he hadn't got overexcited because of the unfortunate event.

The previous evening the sergeant had had a vague feeling – though since he had been in festive mood, he had thought no more about it – that there was something weighing on Anni's mind. It couldn't just be Rechsteiner's

47

illness; that had been going on for three years now and in three years you could get used to a lot of things. It must be something else, something that had happened recently. What? And for the first time it struck him that the landlady of the Hôtel zum Hirschen had not been greatly bothered by the murder. True, in the immediate aftermath she'd asked the sergeant to start the investigation, giving as her reason her fear that the guests might stay away. After that she'd not shown any further interest in the case. Of course, she'd had plenty to occupy her with Fräulein Loppacher. But it was clear that the pressure the woman was under still had not gone away – and Studer had the feeling the pressure had nothing to do with the murder.

While he had been cogitating, Anni had replied, but the words had gone in one ear and out of the other.

"What?" he asked, and Frau Rechsteiner repeated, louder than the first time, that Karl had slept well after the initial excitement. Of course, the doctor had prescribed him a sleeping draught. If only he didn't sweat so much during the night! It did so weaken him. The doctor had prescribed something for that as well – and it worked, but it was a strong poison.

Studer had no idea himself why he had started at the word "poison", as if he'd been stung by a wasp, but he didn't show it and, his mouth full, turned back to Krock.

"So it's Graf you have in mind, the man with the bicycle shop? Jealousy the motive? You could be right," he said musingly. "But that would be another blow for your employee, Herr Krock. Just at the moment Fräulein Loppacher's in love with Ernst Graf. I last saw her a quarter of an hour ago, in Graf's workshop."

"The silly goose!" The final "s" came out as a long hiss.

"A silly goose? Oh, no," said Studer mildly. "I have to admit that as a rule I can't stand women who paint themselves, and when they go so far as to paint their fingernails like Negro women – by the way, did you know that fashion came from Africa? A friend told me who'd spent a long time out there – it really gets my goat." The last expression was a somewhat blunt dialect phrase that sounded odd at the end of a sentence in formal German. "But I'm sure that has nothing to do with her qualities. Or am I wrong?"

"No. In general Fräulein Loppacher's very competent. I'd just hoped that one day she would marry my assistant."

"And your Herr Stieger, was he a good worker?" Studer asked. Instead of waiting for an answer, however, he stood up and went to join a group of people standing in the doorway.

Under Herr Krock's mocking gaze, he first greeted his

wife with two smacking kisses on each cheek, then his daughter had to submit to a similar unaccustomed display of affection. He gave Albert, his son-in-law, a long shake of the hand and his mother, aunts and uncles received the same treatment. He was so much the honest, affectionate family man that Krock whispered some remark to Frau Rechsteiner. Both laughed.

That did not escape the notice of the sergeant from Bern. He gave his son-in-law a slight nod, surreptitiously drawing his attention to the pair by the piano. "Keep an eye on them," he murmured. Albert stared, uncomprehending, and Studer shrugged his massive shoulders. He must have overestimated the abilities of the Thurgau rural gendarmerie.

* * *

At nine Dr Salvisberg, the doctor who was treating Herr Rechsteiner, came. First of all he went upstairs, to examine his patient, then he demanded to see the body of Jean Stieger. At ten the proper authorities arrived: Dr Schläpfer, the examining magistrate, together with his clerk, and Chief of Police Zuberbühler with two detectives.

That meant that the three carriages could set off for Arbon with the wedding party – two uncles, three aunts, the two mothers and the newly wed wife – leaving Sergeant Studer and his son-in-law behind in the hotel.

Studer's wife Hedy had promised to get together whatever was necessary and send it up to Schwarzenstein: photographic plates, printing frames, developer, intensifier and – above all! – summer clothes. Studer couldn't stand it in his black suit any more.

Albert had complained. He didn't want to stay. He'd only got married the previous day, he said, and he was to abandon his wife already? There was a discussion about the matter. A very short discussion. Sergeant Studer had a way of saying "And I need you", which made it very difficult to protest. So Albert had accepted his fate.

At four in the afternoon the magistrate and his group left. Immediately prior to that they had arrested Ernst Graf, dealer in bicycles, born 3 March 1887 in Trogen in the canton of Appenzell AusserRhoden, on suspicion of the wilful murder of Jean Stieger, clerical assistant, born 28 August 1900, resident in St Gallen, 25 Bahnhofstrasse.

When she heard that, Fräulein Martha Loppacher, a secretary with Joachim Krock Private Investigators, gave up her room in the Hôtel zum Hirschen and moved into Graf's bicycle workshop. Frau Anni Rechsteiner-Ibach had agreed to rent out a bed to Fräulein Loppacher.

At six o'clock Fritz Graf, the brother of the arrested man, appeared in the hamlet of Schwarzenstein. He was a crooked little man with a hunchback and twisted features. Fritz Graf also moved into his brother's house.

At seven o'clock Johannes Küng, stableman at the Hôtel zum Hirschen, collected a case from the post office which had been sent express and was addressed to Herr Jakob Studer.

At a quarter past eight three men were eating in the large dining room of the hotel. They were all wearing grey trousers and had rolled up their shirtsleeves. After the meal, at half past precisely, Herr Joachim Krock, owner of an Information Bureau in St Gallen, got up, stretched and went over to the piano. He played four bars and fell off the stool.

There was foam at the corners of his mouth, his eyes were wide open and the pupils so dilated the iris was almost invisible. Studer picked up the elegantly dressed businessman, who was shaking with convulsions, and, with the help of his son-in-law, carried him up to his room.

But when the doctor arrived fifteen minutes later, Joachim Krock was already dead. Dr Salvisberg established that the cause of death was poisoning.

Visiting the Sick

At first when you went into the room you didn't see the sick man, since the head of the bed was right beside the door, only separated from it by a little table with bottles of medicine and boxes of pills. Opening the door, you had the impression you were stepping outside: a huge glass door, reaching from the floor to the ceiling, opened onto a balcony with a view far out over the countryside. In the distance was the gleam of Lake Constance.

If, after entering the room, you were to obey the military command "Left about turn", you would be standing facing the bed and have on your left the bedside table with its collection of medicines and, beside it, the head of Karl Rechsteiner, landlord of the Hôtel zum Hirschen. The top of the bed was against one wall and the side against another, which, however, was interrupted by a window, so that the sick man only had to stretch out his hand to raise the catch and open the window.

Studer went in after Dr Salvisberg and, as he had been the previous day, was horrified at the way Rechsteiner looked. A thin face, the right side smaller than the left, like a waning moon; the nose jutting out sharply; his eyes bright, light brown like unripe hazelnuts. They were staring straight ahead, fixed – and they remained fixed. If the patient wanted to look in a different direction, he turned his head – to the right, to the left – or he raised it and lowered it. He spoke in a whine.

What did they want from him now? "Oh morning, doctor, *salut*, Studer. Take a seat. I'm not well today. My pulse! And my heart!" His kidneys were hurting again too. "Jeeesus, 'm I in pain!"

His hands scrabbled around on the cover, recalling sea creatures, crabs. It was impossible to imagine there was any flesh between the skin and the bones; the skin must be directly attached to the bones, making it look hard and brittle, like the shell of a crustacean.

Dr Salvisberg did not sit down. He began rummaging around among the medicines on the bedside table, picking up one, then another, then another. He pulled out the drawer, scattering boxes as he searched. Finally he looked up and asked where the pills were he'd prescribed Rechsteiner to stop him sweating at night.

How thin under his nightshirt were the shoulders he shrugged! Then he turned his face to the right – and since his eyes were in the shade, they seemed darker, as dark as moist clay.

"Dunno . . . I've no idea."

"What were they, Doctor?" Studer asked, slipping, like Rechsteiner, into Swiss German.

Dr Salvisberg sat down and crossed his legs, his left hand grasping his ankle while his right arm hung slackly over the back of the chair.

"A mixture," he said quietly. "Atropine and hyoscine."

"Deadly nightshade and henbane," Studer muttered.

The doctor looked at him in surprise. "'Pon my soul, Sergeant, I'd no idea you knew about poisons. Where did you learn all that?"

Studer sat there in his favourite posture, leaning forward slightly, forearms on thighs, hands clasped. That was neither here nor there, he said. The point was, he knew about them and, seeing the dead man's dilated pupils, he'd immediately thought of the poisons the doctor had just mentioned.

Dr Salvisberg gave the Bern detective a suspicious look, recalling that this Studer's behaviour towards the senior investigating officers had been distinctly odd. True, the examining magistrate had treated the sergeant with a certain degree of respect and a great deal of tolerance and accepted everything he'd done: moving the body into the hotel cellar, interrogating Johannes Küng without authorization, visiting Ernst Graf. The chief of Appenzell Canton police had actually listened attentively when Studer had maintained that Graf was innocent. And the examining magistrate had been almost apologetic when he'd said the sergeant was probably right, he too had the impression there was more to this case than appeared on the surface, but . . . but . . . the wheel the spoke fitted had been found in his workshop, there was no doubt the hair on the strange murder weapon came from Graf's dog, and the man had admitted he had been jealous of Stieger. And he had no alibi . . .

"Alibi!" Studer had said in a rather contemptuous tone. "You people and your alibis! How do you expect a man who lives alone to prove he was at home?"

On top of all that, the magistrate went on, the groom from the hotel had seen Graf hanging round the building the previous evening.

The whole scene went through the doctor's mind as he stared at the sergeant's bowed head. From the bed came the voice of the sick man asking if something else had happened.

"No, no," the doctor reassured him, "it's just a friendly visit – isn't it?" Studer nodded. "I just wanted to make sure the medicine to stop you sweating during the night is still here."

"Did you have many visitors this afternoon?" Studer asked without looking at Rechsteiner.

The police, that was all, and they hadn't stayed for long. But he had found it tiring. Then Fräulein Loppacher had come around six to say goodbye. She'd told him she was moving over into Graf's house. *Someone* had to look after the poor animals.

"Did Fräulein Loppacher stay for long?" Studer asked.

"A quarter of an hour," was the reply, "a quarter of an hour, no more."

"Where did she sit?"

Rechsteiner pointed to the chair where Studer was sitting.

"Did she touch your medicines?"

That he couldn't say. He'd been staring out of the window all of the time, the clouds over the hills were so beautiful, like molten silver.

"And no one else came to see you?"

"Anni popped in once or twice to see how I was – Oh yes, now I remember. There was another visit, a strange one, someone I'd never have expected to see here in my sickroom."

"Herr Krock?" Studer asked, but Rechsteiner shook his head slowly.

"No, no. It was Graf's brother, he was suddenly here in the room. I didn't even hear the door because I'd just opened the window to let in the evening breeze. All at once someone was bending over me and at first I didn't recognize his face. It's such a long time since Fritz Graf left Schwarzenstein, five years, I think – before I fell ill. He had an argument with Ernst and went to St Gallen, worked in a factory there. And suddenly there he was in my room.

"'What d'you want, Fritz?' I asked him. 'Sit down. Pity about Ernst,' I said. 'And all because of a woman. A shame, a real shame.'

"At that Fritz laughed. He didn't say anything, just laughed and went to the door. Then he turned round. 'I just wanted to see how you were, Rechsteiner,' he said. 'Can you still walk?' Then he closed the door behind him without waiting for an answer."

"Two visitors," Studer summarized. "Fräulein Loppacher and Graf's brother."

The doctor was looking at the bedside table again. Suddenly he said, "I've told you before, Rechsteiner, you shouldn't take so much of the sleeping draught. It's harmful. I brought you a bottle the day before yesterday and already it's half-empty. That's not very sensible."

Rechsteiner's face crumpled, as if he was about to cry, but then a voice said, "Don't keep going on at my husband, Doctor. If you knew how badly he sleeps at night – and it's not just his fault; I was so upset yesterday, I took some myself."

Anni was in the room and Studer couldn't understand how she'd got there, as he was sitting right next to the door that led out into the corridor. But when he looked round, he saw that there was a handle on the wall at right angles to the balcony door. So there was another door there! It was almost invisible, being covered from top to bottom in the same paper as the wall itself. Studer stood up, pushed past the woman and turned the handle.

A second bedroom, but dark, just a tiny window in one corner. A narrow iron bedstead, a table with a comb and hairbrush, a book beside them. Studer picked it up. He smiled. It wasn't a book; it was a slim pamphlet in green covers. It was a popular herbal. Better not let the doctor see it! Studer replaced it with the title page down and tiptoed back out of the room.

Then the two men said goodbye to Rechsteiner and left. Studer just had time to whisper to Anni that he'd see her in fifteen minutes, down below, outside. She nodded. Her face was pale, her eyes glassy. As was understandable.

Once they were in the corridor, Studer asked whether it was possible the medicine that had disappeared had been used to poison Joachim Krock.

"I usually prepare my medicines myself," the doctor

replied, "but those pills were an exception. I sent the prescription to the chemist in Heiden. They were tiny sugared pills, Sergeant, each containing about a thousandth of a gram of each of the poisons. In all there were about a hundred pills. As any schoolboy knows, one-thousandth times a hundred is a tenth. And a tenth of a gram would have certainly been sufficient."

Studer nodded. That left the question of how the poison had been administered. In Krock's food? No, because in that case he and Albert would have had it too.

"As far as I know, hyoscine's tasteless. What about atropine?"

"It has a faint bitter taste."

Bitter? Had the businessman from St Gallen eaten anything with a bitter taste. Chocolate? *Chabis*. Bitter? What was there that was bitter? Suddenly the sergeant slapped himself on the forehead.

* * *

He could see the scene clearly in his mind's eye:

The dining room with the table by the piano set for three. At each place is a glass with a transparent brown liquid.

"What's that?" he asks the waitress who had wiped her

floor cloth on the trousers of his black Sunday suit that morning.

"Vermouth," she replies.

Krock is sitting at the piano playing a waltz, so slow and sad it sounds like one of the Salvation Army's penitential hymns. Ottilia puts the bowls of soup on the table, goes up to Krock and tells him dinner is served. Studer has his back to the table, his hands are full. Krock stands up, looks at Studer, looks at Albert, picks up his glass: "*Prost.*" – "Your very good health." – "Your health."

The glasses clink, a few drops of the brown liquid fall onto the tablecloth.

Soup; cold roast meat; salad; strawberries – dinner's over in fifteen minutes. Krock gets up and goes over to the piano. He hadn't closed the lid and the keys are a shimmer of white in the gathering darkness. He sits down on the swivel chair. Does he sway? No, the sergeant's probably imagining that. His hairless white hands descend on the keys in a powerful chord. That morning's funeral march . . .

And then he's on the floor, doubled up, foam forming at the corners of his mouth, his pupils so dilated they've swallowed up the irises. The sergeant and his son-in-law carry the dead man up to his room and gently lay him down on the bed.

* * *

"Just a moment, Doctor," Studer murmured, "I just need to go and have a quick look at something."

He jumped down the stairs, three at a time, and arrived breathless in the kitchen. He stood in the doorway and looked round the room. No sink. He hurried past the large stove, past the skinny cook, who stared at him in astonishment. Correct! The door led to the scullery.

Dirty dishes: plates, bowls . . . And the glasses? There they were, all three of them, in a dark corner. And they hadn't been washed yet. Studer went back into the kitchen, asked for a sheet of newspaper and wrapped the glasses up carefully in it. Carefully – making sure he only held the glasses by the foot, between thumb and forefinger.

Then he went back up the stairs, slowly, stowed the package in his suitcase and went to room no. 7.

Blotting Paper and a Conversation

The bed on which the dead body lay was a proper hotel bed with brass bedposts with balls on the top reflecting the light from the lamp fixed to the ceiling. Albert was beside the open suitcase, the contents of which he had spread out neatly on the table by the window. Studer, hands clasped behind his back, examined the objects. Nothing interesting: a lot of little bottles and tubes; a Gillette razor, silver-plated, a shaving brush and cream, a nail file, scissors. On the bed was a pair of blue silk pyjamas with bright red trimming. What surprised the sergeant most of all was the complete lack of papers: no documents, no letters, nothing.

This observation did not fit in with another: on the table was a fountain pen with the cap off, and it lay beside the desk pad as if the writer had just put it down for a moment.

The desk pad – the blotter! Studer took it to the middle of the room and let the full light fall on it. The top sheet was new and a few letters could be made out. Letters in green ink. Studer picked up the fountain pen carefully and scribbled a few letters in his notebook. The pen had green ink, the same colour as the blotted letters on the desk pad. He fetched the mirror that hung above the washbasin, placed the desk pad on the bed – because that was where the light was best – and held the mirror upright behind it.

The letters, thick and underlined as well, must be part of an address. He could make out an "a", then a group, "nhe" and, as part of the same word, an "m". He wrote down the legible letters, separating them with full stops. The result was: ".a.nhe.m".

The sergeant stared at the mirror again. Above the line of letters he'd noted down, which probably belonged to the name of a town, there was another. It was very faint; the green ink seemed to dry very quickly. He could decipher "..ie...f.p.lic.". In the top corner of the blotter, above the signature ("J. Krock", very clear, surrounded by a flowing flourish) were two words: "forged", "cheque" and two rows of numbers. One began with a 3 or a 5, which was not very clear, followed by four zeros. So, 30,000 or 50,000. The second row was a year: 1924, though it wasn't absolutely clear whether the last digit was a 4 or a 7.

Deduction? Herr Joachim Krock had spent the afternoon writing a letter. Where was it? In the post?

It was with a slight shock that Studer suddenly realized he was no longer holding the mirror. But still it was upright. Without noticing, the sergeant had leaned it against the stiff legs of the dead man.

* * *

On the slope that went up behind the hotel was a huge lime tree. It was past ten already and yet the day seemed unwilling to yield to night. The air was still aglitter with particles of light and a cloud over Lake Constance looked like a fat man who was celebrating the midsummer festival by wearing a dark-red waistcoat that was stretched tight over his paunch.

Anni was silent. Then she raised her hand to the back of her head. A simple gesture, but it immediately took the sergeant back to the distant past . . . A small schoolroom, boys on one side, girls on the other. In the front desk Anni Ibach is bent low over her slate, writing away. It seems to Köbu Studer that he can hear the scratch of *one* pencil from among the scratching of all the other pencils. Suddenly she puts her slate-pencil down and lifts her hand up to the back of her head. Anni was seven and Köbu Studer eight. He wasn't the brightest in the school, nowhere near as clever as Anni. And now they'd met again.

In those days they'd trotted home from school together and sometimes Köbu had protected Anni from the attacks of other boys. It was his mother's fault, always telling her son he should protect the weak. Could his mother's constant preaching have been one reason why Studer had joined the police? Perhaps. He'd imagined he'd be able to help the poor, shield children from abuse, women from their husbands. How differently things had turned out!

"Remember, Anni?" Studer said in his homely dialect, "All those years ago in Rickenbach?"

Anni nodded, then suddenly burst into tears.

"Now, now," the sergeant said, permitting himself a gentle pat on her bowed back. "Come on, Anni. What's wrong? There's no need to cry."

But the sobbing went on. Studer heaved a deep sigh and looked up at the first stars, hardly daring to come out, still in shock from the overlong day. The sobs grew quieter and Studer gently asked what it was that made her take on so. The second death? Anni nodded vigorously, she couldn't speak yet; it was as if the tears had been held back for a long time. It had been one heartache after another and the woman had bottled it all up inside herself. But now it had all come out and the outburst was doing her good.

Studer had taken hold of her hand, a firm hand which felt cool, slightly rough on the palm – that came from all her hard work. But there were white threads in her hair, which in his memory the man still saw as dark brown, like old wood, lots of fine white threads, shimmering, like the threads that float through the air on sunny autumn days.

"He torments me so," she said quietly. She undid her cuff, pulled the sleeve back and pointed at two marks. They looked black in the twilight. If she didn't do everything Rechsteiner wanted, she said, he pinched her arm.

"It's because he's ill," Anni said. "The illness's made him so irritable. He used to be a big, strong man; who'd have thought he'd end up like this? I met him at a wedding in St Gallen. We got on well together. He'd just come back from Germany and I was housekeeper in a hotel. He suggested we should do something together, run a hotel somewhere out in the country; there was one for sale in Schwarzenstein. Neither of us was a spring chicken, it wasn't a grand passion, you know, Köbu, but we got on well together and at first everything was fine. Until he fell ill. Now it's unbearable."

She stopped. Studer couldn't bring himself to ask any questions. She looked up. She had a broad, full face with a straight forehead that was very white. The lower part was already showing signs of fat – indeed the beginnings of a double chin were clearly visible – but it didn't matter. Behind the woman's face the sergeant still saw the features of the little girl who had trotted home with him, hand in hand. Such things, once aroused, didn't simply return to their slumbers.

"From Germany?" Studer asked after a while. "Which town had he been in?"

She couldn't remember; somewhere in Baden, she thought. She sighed. Her problems with Rechsteiner wouldn't be half so bad if it hadn't been for the business with Otti and the business with the Loppacher woman.

Studer pricked up his ears. Did she want to tell him about it?

There wasn't much to tell. What had happened with the Eyetie was that Rechsteiner had ordered Ottilia to keep her under surveillance. His own wife! Every Saturday evening the waitress had to go to his bedside with all the week's bills and receipts, and Anni had had to stand there and listen to his criticisms: this was wrong and that was wrong and why hadn't she charged that guest more? Then Rechsteiner added up the takings and sent his wife out. Later Otti usually had a bundle of letters to take to the post. And when Fräulein Loppacher had come, Rechsteiner had made her his secretary. Whole afternoons she'd heard the clatter of the typewriter in his room, sometimes until eleven o'clock at night, until midnight. Impossible to get to sleep! Afterwards Rechsteiner would get her out of bed two or three times

– and she still had to get up at five in the morning. Studer could imagine: four cows in the stall, two horses for the carriage, pigs, poultry. Sometimes she'd gone haymaking just to get out of the house – for years she hadn't had a holiday, not even a Sunday off. Sometimes she'd thought of ending it all, but that was easier said than done.

"Anneli!" Studer said.

A cool breeze from the lake sprang up and the sergeant shivered. The leaves of the lime tree rustled and a few flowers that had already opened came swirling down. One stuck in Anni's hair.

So there he was, a man who'd devoted his whole life to the so-called science of criminology. What use was it? Now? Sitting next to a woman in tears? The first requirement of the science was to ask questions and the second to be objective. Objective? Put simply, that meant uninvolved. But how did these scientific gentlemen do that, remain uninvolved when your childhood suddenly came back to you and you saw your old classroom again, and the way home and your mother? There'd been a lime tree behind his father's house too, and in the summer a high ladder was placed up against it and a boy and a girl had picked lime blossom.

And now? Now he was an old man. Hedy had been a good wife to him; the only thing he might say against her was that he hadn't picked lime blossom with *her* but with another girl. As a trained detective he ought to be asking questions. Objective questions? There was no way he could do that. Though he had learned one thing: Rechsteiner had been in Germany.

"Can you really not remember which town Rechsteiner lived in before he came to St Gallen?" Studer asked. "In Baden? Think!"

"He told me there were two rivers met there – and there was a big bridge connecting the town to another. And it had a harbour, a big harbour. If you say a name I could tell you if it's right."

The summer evening was so quiet and peaceful he had to force himself to think. He would much rather have thought of nothing and just filled his eyes with the quivering light of the stars, the velvety darkness of the woods, over there, on the side of the hill, and the hard black of the distant lake.

Two rivers, a harbour, a bridge across the Rhine . . . he ought to know it. Offenburg? No. Karlsruhe? No. And Mainz wasn't in Baden.

Studer took a long leather case out of his pocket, pulled the straw out of the Brissago, placed his notebook open on his knee then lit the cigar.

In the light of the flame he read: ".anhe.m".

He hadn't given any more thought to the puzzle, but now, suddenly, the solution appeared before his eyes in the light of the burning straw:

"*Mannheim.*"

He almost shouted it out, so that Anni placed her hand on his sleeve. Of course it was Mannheim, she said, but that was no reason to make such a noise.

Studer apologized. He'd only cried out so loud because he'd burned his fingers with the match. It was instead of a swearword. The Krauts said, "Good Lord of Mannheim!" Didn't they?

And the sergeant was happy to see a smile appear on the broad face (oh yes, the double chin was clearly visible) with cheeks that were still moist. Her lips parted, little wrinkles appeared at the corners of her eyes – and then she laughed. A shy laugh, a laugh that made him feel sad because it was no more than an attempt to remember something she had long forgotten, had grown unaccustomed to.

Mannheim? Why had Joachim Krock, owner of an information bureau in St Gallen, written a letter, on the day he died, to the town in Baden where Karl Rechsteiner, owner of the Hôtel zum Hirschen, had made his money?

Studer stood up, stretched, offered his arm to Anni and the two strolled back together to the large building rising up out of the darkness before them. There was only one window lit, on the first floor. As they came closer they could hear the clatter of a typewriter – "Fräulein" Loppacher was at work for the sick man.

Suddenly Studer asked a question (it had fluttered into his mind, silent and dark, like a bat): "Can Rechsteiner still walk?"

They were so close to the hotel that he whispered, for fear he might be heard through the open window. The answer also came in a whisper: "Both legs are paralysed. You can ask the doctor." A hand took his, squeezed it. "Thanks, Köbu." And the woman was gone.

The sergeant walked up and down outside the back door, up and down. For half an hour, an hour. The clock on the tower in Schwarzenstein struck midnight. The clatter in the patient's room broke off. Studer stopped. Footsteps on the stairs, a door opening. A white dress was a bright spot in the dark, then merged with the whitewashed wall.

"Good evening, Fräulein Loppacher," said Studer in his best formal German. "May I see you home?"

A little suppressed exclamation, then: "Certainly, if it gives you pleasure, Sergeant."

The stress was on "sergeant". Not Herr Studer, no: "sergeant". Just as you might say "porter" or "driver".

The Brother

As Studer walked along silently beside the typist, he recalled the second row of letters he had written down in his notebook: "..ie...f.p.lic." He felt like slapping his forehead again. Any schoolboy would have guessed that the last part was "police"! Which meant that the first part must be "chief of". That left the question of why Herr Joachim Krock had written to the Chief of Police in Mannheim. Was there a connection with the regular correspondence between a certain Fräulein, who was a guest at the hotel, and Jean Stieger? The sergeant automatically patted his inside jacket pocket. Yes, the envelopes were still there. And Studer sighed at the thought that he would not get much sleep that night. Plates, printing frames, fixative and intensifier were waiting for him in his room. He had to show that he hadn't forgotten the things he had learned in the "scientific" forensic laboratory of Dr Locard in Lyons.

What had he learned there? He had learned that every sheet of paper that has been pressed down on a blank sheet for long enough will leave traces on that second sheet which are invisible to the naked eye, but become visible on a photographic plate after having been copied ten or twelve times. The only problem was, it was one hell of a slog. A good job he'd made sure he had a bottle of pure alcohol – not to drink, not that state-controlled rotgut, but to dry the plates, it was quite good for that.

But that was to come later. For the moment it would be a good idea to find out a bit more about the two people who were playing the hermit in a mechanic's workshop. It wasn't going to be easy.

And it turned out to be even more difficult than Studer had imagined. He was given a friendly welcome, though. Fritz Graf, the brother of the man who'd been arrested on suspicion of murder, gave the sergeant's hand a long and vigorous shake, at the same time dancing around like a dervish. He contorted his skinny limbs and pulled incredible faces, while his little, crafty eyes kept looking past Studer's head. His greeting was breathless.

"A . . . a . . . ha . . . th . . . the . . . shaa . . . ser . . . ge . . . hant's . . . hhee . . . here." He withdrew his hand and scuttled round the room, not like a normal person, but sideways, as if his right shoulder were his chest; as he went, he crossed his legs, as if he were practising complicated dance steps. He brought a chair. "Sissit . . . sissit dohown, sir. Tha . . . thhaat's it."

He himself went over to the workbench, placed his hands flat on it, heaved himself up and sat there, swinging his legs, alternately fast and slow; his right shoulder still stuck out in front. There was the glow of a coal fire in the forge. Fritz Graf did not appear to register the presence of Martha Loppacher. Since he didn't offer her a chair, she sat down on a bed that had been put up in one of the corners, opposite the forge. The case with the typewriter in it was on the floor.

Studer wondered why Fräulein Loppacher, a typist, had written her letters to Jean Stieger by hand. He still didn't know what to make of the young woman with her war paint. Joachim Krock had called her a silly goose. So it was understandable that she'd fallen in love with Ernst Graf. At first she'd probably just made sheep's eyes at him. And then? Had the man perhaps grasped his opportunity? The sergeant wouldn't have put it past him. He lived together with his animals. His animals loved him . . . Loved? . . . What else did that mean than that the dark bicycle dealer exercised a certain attraction over all living creatures? Perhaps scientists would have talked of "magnetism" – not modern scientists; their predecessors. And was not Martha Loppacher a creature like Mousie the sheep? A creature with a diploma from commercial college, hammering out the dictation on her machine? But that work, if one could call it work, could at best be compared to the chimpanzees riding bicycles in Basel Zoo. A skill acquired by drill that bypassed her birdbrain. Anni was quite a different person. Brave, intelligent . . .

Such were the idle thoughts going through the sergeant's mind as he sat watching Fritz Graf's legs swing to and fro.

"Why have you given up your job in St Gallen?" Studer asked.

"Bebe . . . bebe . . . cause . . ." Pause. Incredible the way the man could twist his lips. They were like strips of red rubber. They stretched and shrank, stretched and shrank. Sometimes his mouth was so big, it looked as if it was going to swallow up his ears, then it became tiny and round. "Bebe . . . bebecause . . ." That was all he could get out, but the sergeant had the feeling his stammering wasn't natural – or at least that under certain circumstances the man could speak quite normally, calmly. But under what circumstances?

Finally, after many attempts, Fritz managed to explain he'd heard of his brother's arrest from Herr Krock.

"From Herr Krock?" Studer asked dubiously.

For the first time an answer came from the bed. Fritz Graf, Martha Loppacher informed him in her somewhat simplistic formal German, was the office messenger.

76

"Ye . . . yeyes. Mmm . . . messen . . . mmessen . . . ger."

Aha, a messenger. For Herr Krock. Studer blew his nose loudly, then changed his tactics. He left Fritz Graf in peace and turned to the typist.

"Fräulein Loppacher," he said, "I've been wanting to ask you various things for some time. But I have to tell you that I have no right to insist you answer. I'm only looking into the case because I promised Frau Rechsteiner and also because I firmly believe your friend is innocent."

"Yeye . . . yes. Ernscht is innn . . . inno . . . cent," Fritz Graf croaked.

"Just shut up for a moment, chatterbox," Studer said in the friendly tones of his Swiss dialect. For Fräulein Loppacher he reverted to formal German. "To help me prove that, you'll have to be open with me and answer a few questions. Are you willing?"

Martha Loppacher nodded and said: "Yes."

"Good. What's in the letters Rechsteiner dictates to you?"

The young woman stood up, opened the case of the portable typewriter and handed the sergeant several sheets of paper. Carbons. Studer read them quickly. Enquiries to banks, commission agencies, well-known loan sharks who had so far evaded the police (Studer recognized a few of the names and addresses). Requests for loans:

three thousand, five thousand, two thousand. The hotel was offered as security. The only burden on it, the letters claimed, was the original mortgage. Why was Rechsteiner doing all this behind his wife's back? Why did a sick man need all that money?

"And the other letters? The letters you wrote a week ago yesterday?"

They'd all said the same.

"And the letters you wrote to Stieger?"

Silence. Studer couldn't see the woman's face; it was in the shadow. The only light, a very bright bulb hanging over the workbench, had a shade that threw the light down onto the bench, leaving the corners of the room in darkness. The spanners, chisels and pliers gleamed, but all that could be seen on the bed in the corner was an indistinct patch of white – Fräulein Loppacher's dress.

She sat there in silence for a long time. Eventually Studer realized what the cause of her silence was and sent Fritz Graf out, telling him to have a look at the animals and then go to bed.

"Yeye . . . yes . . . Sesese . . . Serge . . . ant."

The door opened. The moon was spilling its frozen light over the yard and in it the scrap iron took on eerie forms. The barrel hoops looked like the wheels of some fairy-tale carriage and the tangled wire like huge insects with thin legs and gigantic feelers. The door closed – and the sergeant felt a gentle touch on his knee. He looked under the table. Two shimmering eyes were fixed on him; a light-grey paw was raised and gently placed on his thigh. Then a dull drum roll was heard: Bruin was wagging his tail and it was thumping against an empty petrol can.

"Yes, you're a good dog." The sergeant gently stroked its pointed head. A thought came to him and, as he couldn't get it out of his head, he said to the dog: "Yes, Bruin. Later."

Fräulein Loppacher emerged from her corner. As Fritz Graf had done not that long ago, she placed her hands on the workbench, pushed herself up and sat on it. She too swung her legs, not three feet from Studer's nose. And it was seductive, for there was no denying it: the girl had lovely legs.

Staring at the floor between his splayed thighs, the sergeant repeated his question. Then he raised his head and looked Martha Loppacher straight in the eye. She did not lower her gaze.

Every two days she'd sent the copies of Rechsteiner's letters to St Gallen, she explained quietly. Her illness and the rest cure, she went on after a pause, had just been a pretext. What had happened was this: six weeks ago Herr Krock had received a letter from Rechsteiner. What did it say? Almost word for word the same as the letters the sergeant had just read. Herr Krock thought there was money to be made and had sent her to Schwarzenstein to spy out the land.

After the initial letter, Herr Krock had made enquiries about the hotel. The results were encouraging. No debts. The interest on the mortgage was always paid promptly. But Joachim Krock also learned that Rechsteiner had written to other money dealers in St Gallen, always requesting a small loan. As in those letters there. Two thousand francs, three thousand, in two cases only a thousand. "There's something going on here," Herr Krock had said and had sent her to have a look round. But he had told her to address the letters to Stieger, so as not to arouse suspicions in the village.

Studer could still feel the warmth of the dog's head on his knee, and it kept prodding him with its snout, as if Bruin wanted to remind the tall, well-built man of something: "Don't forget my master."

So little had Studer forgotten that he suddenly changed his tactics and asked, in his thickest Bernese dialect: "Tell me, girl, why did you take up with Ernst Graf?"

Martha Loppacher's hair was definitely bleached. Such a delicate blond colour couldn't be natural. And it was waved too. But the blush that spread over the girl's cheeks was clearly to be seen – no, she hadn't powdered her face that evening – as was the fear that filled her eyes. And Studer could have bet that the tongue she passed over her lips was dry, like her mouth, like her throat.

There was no answer. And Studer found a bizarre thought going through his mind; the girl's brain, he thought, must have permanent waves like her hair. Permanent waves? Her feelings had been set in one particular shape. The girl couldn't see a man without automatically "falling" in love as the English put it. It could be with a sick man (like Rechsteiner), a semi-savage (like Graf) or her superior (like Stieger). But who was the stylist who'd done that to her brain? He – or rather it – wasn't hard to find. It wasn't a person: it was a spirit that could take on different forms and speak in different tongues. It flickered across the screen in the cinema, it sang in operettas and popular songs, it spoke out of novels in the voice of the lord's son, the junior doctor, the countess. And it was like a magic spell: its singing turned the heart to stone, its dancing hardened the mind and its chatter put the emotions in curlers – what was left but permanent waves in the brain? And the saddest thing about it was that one couldn't blame Martha for painting and polishing her soul like her fingernails. Perhaps she'd danced with Stieger a few times, let him kiss her – and then she found herself faced with a dead body. And like an automaton carrying out the prescribed movements, she flings herself over the dead man (as she's seen so often in the cinema), crying "My beloved!"

However, salvation did still seem possible. The fact that Martha Loppacher, who certainly considered herself the opposite of tender-hearted, had suddenly blushed, suggested that she was not indifferent to the strange fellow that was Ernst Graf. When she replied it was in her homely dialect, not her formal German.

"I like him, Herr Studer."

There it was, then. After all, he wasn't supposed to be helping a little lost lamb find her way. Really? Was he supposed to do nothing but pursue criminal investigations? Studer shook his head. Then he asked Martha whether her parents were still alive. No, she said, her parents had died ten years ago and she'd had to look after herself. The money she'd inherited had been just enough for a few years at commercial college, for the exam and the diploma.

Was it an illusion? The sergeant had the feeling the permanent waves were slowly, very slowly, losing their rigid shape. Not the visible ones, they remained, not a hair out of place, but the others . . . Were those painted lips twitching? Were the corners of her mouth turning down? And weren't there two tears rolling down past her nose, and two more and then more and more?

Gently Studer asked Martha whether she couldn't understand how difficult it was for the landlady if a woman, an outsider, came between her and her husband? Shared secrets with him? Would she, Martha, promise to stop playing at being Rechsteiner's secretary?

A vigorous nod.

Again the dog drummed softly with its tail on the can, waking Studer from his thoughts. He noticed two things.

The first seemed relatively unimportant. The girl was staring into space, dry-eyed. But the fear in her eyes and contorted features was clear, almost tangible.

The second seemed even less important. Martha Loppacher had leaned back and taken a file out of one of the leather hangers. Then she opened the vice, placed a nail between the jaws and tightened them. And then she began to file the nail. Mindlessly.

She held the file in her right hand, bracing it with her left and taking long strokes, like a trained mechanic.

Studer recalled that the spoke from a bicycle wheel that had been embedded so deep in Jean Stieger's body had been filed to a point. For the first time it struck him that no great strength was needed to kill someone with a weapon like that.

The scrape-scrape-scrape of the file.

"Stop it!" Studer barked at her. The monotonous rasping

was unbearable. It had also spoilt the mood. Studer stood up and said, not looking up, "Get off to bed. Goodnight." Without thinking, he had reverted to formal German.

He went out into the yard. And the dog came with him, as if it were the most natural thing in the world. The sergeant hadn't called it or clicked his fingers to tell it to follow him.

The Brother (continued)

The Pomeranian led the way, though it wasn't actually necessary. The door was slightly ajar and a faint light shone through the cracks. As Studer pushed it open, the light went out. A voice came from the corner where Ernst Graf had been lying in bed that morning. Did the sergeant mind sitting in the dark? Talking was easier in the dark; it was only in the light, when people were watching his lips, that he began to stammer. It seemed to be true, for the man in the dark corner talked fluently, in a soft voice the sergeant had not yet heard. No croaking, no breathless repetition of scraps of words.

Studer felt his way across the room. The moonlight reached as far as the middle, then it was pitch dark. His foot hit something soft. There was a loud, penetrating squeak. "Shh, Ideli," came the voice from the bed. The piglet snorted, rustled its straw. Then it fell silent.

There were no chairs in the room, said the voice; the sergeant would have to make do with the floor. Did he mind sitting on the floor? No?

"Thank you for coming, Sergeant, even though it's late,"

the voice in the darkness went on. "Out there – I know I behave like a little child, but it's not my fault. The reason both of us, Ernst and me, have turned out so odd is because our father used to beat us. He beat everyone and everything when he was drunk: mother, the dog, the horses, the cows. And us. We both grew up to be good workers, but we're afraid of people. I worked in factories, first of all in Arbon, then in St Gallen. But I never stayed long in one place. My workmates used to make fun of me – it was no life, Sergeant. So I grabbed at the chance when Herr Krock offered me a job."

"How did that come about?" Studer asked. He was sitting on a folded blanket that had been pushed over to him without a word. Bruin lay beside him, his head once more on the sergeant's knee.

"It was three months ago. A gentleman came to my room one evening, about eight it would be. Young. With a long nose. To be honest, Sergeant, I didn't like the look of his eyes and mouth, but he started without giving me a chance to say anything. He'd come from my brother in Schwarzenstein, he said. Would I like a job as office messenger? Free board and lodging. A hundred francs a month. I jumped at the opportunity."

Studer was having difficulty concentrating. In his mind's eye he could still see the vice – and two hands with painted fingernails holding a file and filing, filing . . .

86

"I was happy with the job. I was often sent out, to this or that village. I was to talk to the landlords in the inns and keep my ears open for the gossip. Of course, I couldn't report what I'd heard orally, but at school I was always the best at German; I've no problem with writing. So I wrote everything down and gave it to the gentlemen. They were happy with that; in the second month I already had a rise to a hundred and twenty francs. Then I wrote to my brother Ernst, thanking him for getting me the job. He wrote back that that was the first he'd heard of it, but that didn't bother me."

"What kind of firm was it?"

"I never really found out what Herr Krock actually did. Once a lady came – when I wasn't out and about, I stayed in my little room; it was next to the main office and when the bell on the wall rang, I had to go in right away – so a lady I didn't know came, I showed her in and went back to my room, leaving the lady alone with Herr Krock. Suddenly the bell rings. I open the door, go into the office. The lady's there, with her back to me and a gun in her hand. Herr Krock's sitting at his desk, quite calm. I grab the lady's arm, she drops the gun, I pick it up and put in on the desk.

"Herr Krock picked up the gun, tossed it in a drawer and said: 'That makes it three thousand . . .' The lady took a little booklet out of her pocket, tore out a leaf and wrote on it. 'Fritz,' Herr Krock said, 'pop down to the post office, the post office bank. They'll give you some money. Say Frau . . . Frau . . .' – I've forgotten the name, Sergeant – 'Say that Frau . . . Frau whatever sent you.' Three thousand francs, Sergeant, three thousand francs!"

Blackmail? Usury? Was it really so unlikely that a black-mailer (or a usurer) had been going about his business in St Gallen without the police knowing? Or were the St Gallen police aware of it, but had no proof? And Herr Joachim Krock had continued to play the part of a respected member of the community.

"What else did he do in his office?" Studer asked.

"He got a lot of letters. From all over the place. France, England, Germany. I think Herr Krock was a Kraut himself. He used to buy houses too and then sell them. A few times I had to go out into the St Gallen Oberland – by bicycle, Sergeant, bicycle! – to take money to the landlords of inns. I did the same for landlords in the Appenzell region."

"You never came to see Rechsteiner?" Studer asked.

"No, never."

Silence. The moonlight had moved across the room. Now it was by the door. Then a pitter-patter was heard, the pitter-patter of tiny hooves approaching. The door was pushed wide open. The two goats came in and Fritz cried, "Hi kids." The sheep followed hesitantly. "*Salut*, Mousie," he said. The animals Ernst Graf had saved trotted into the room then gathered round the bed, including Studer in their circle. It was like a fairy tale: two brothers, both ugly, the younger perhaps even more unfortunate than the elder; he could only stammer when people were watching his lips. But what do animals care whether a person is handsome or not? They know people better than we bipeds know our brothers and sisters. And Studer felt something like pride that the goats, the sheep and the dog had accepted him.

Fritz Graf asked whether the animals were bothering Studer. He shook his head indignantly – bothering him!? – but then remembered the other could not see him shaking his head, so he said, in a voice he wouldn't have recognized as his own even though it said his favourite word, " Bother me? *Chabis*!" On the contrary, he added, it was a remarkable night, it reminded him of his childhood. As a lad he'd always got on well with animals, and anyway . . . The last words came out a little grumpily and he was surprised to hear Fritz laugh.

"There was one other thing I wanted to ask," Studer said, leaning back comfortably – "Mousie", as the witty brothers called the sheep, had settled behind him so that he had a soft, warm backrest. "When did Krock leave the office?"

"I couldn't say precisely," Fritz replied. "There was a telephone call yesterday afternoon, around five. It was after that that he left the office. He told me to answer the telephone and write down any messages."

The sergeant, surprised, asked him if he could use the telephone.

"Certainly, Sergeant. Then I'm alone and no one's watching my lips."

"Oh, of course. And as office boy, so to speak, you have a room on the premises."

"In my room, the room next to the office, there's a bed and a little table – my clothes are kept in a cupboard out in the corridor. I can hear the telephone very well from there. It rang at seven, a woman asking for Herr Krock. I'd hardly started to answer when she hung up. At eight Herr Krock rang. 'No messages?' – 'No, sir.' It was quiet for the rest of the night. This morning Herr Krock rang again at eight. 'Listen, Fritz, your brother's been arrested because he killed Herr Stieger. Lock up the office and come to Schwarzenstein.' Then he —"

Studer sat up so sharply the sheep behind him gave a quiet baa of pain. "What was the time?" he asked.

"Eight this morning."

"You're sure?"

"Sure, quite sure."

But the police and the examining magistrate hadn't arrived until ten o'clock! They'd arrested Graf at three and only taken him away at four! And Joachim Krock had already known whom they were going to arrest at eight in the morning?

When you thought about it, it didn't exactly take psychic powers to predict his arrest. Hadn't Studer come to the same conclusion himself? Still . . .

"So I set off right away. That is, not right away; first of all I had to tidy up the office, wash and make my bed. After that I made myself some lunch and then I left. I got two punctures on the way, so it was six before I reached Schwarzenstein."

"Who'll carry on Herr Krock's firm now?" Studer asked and he could hear Fritz shrug his shoulders.

"No idea," he said. "There were only the four of us: Stieger and Krock, Fräulein Loppacher and me."

"Goodnight, Fritz. Sleep well." Studer got up carefully, very carefully, so as not to tread on one of the animals.

"G'night, Sergeant. And thanks."

The moon had set. The sky resembled a blackboard that hadn't been properly cleaned, the stars little chalk marks. There was a bank of cloud in the east that looked like a floor cloth that had been used to wipe up some red wine that had been spilt. The *Foehn* was blowing and the air was hot and oppressive. The grass was dry. Panting, the sergeant climbed the slope to the bench under the lime tree, sat down and wiped his head with his handkerchief.

There was no dawn chorus. The stars had gone. Instead there were wisps of white stuck to the sky, lit by the rising sun. The lake was gleaming like hot tar.

The sergeant looked up and down the road. There was something that ought to be there, but he couldn't think what it was. What was missing? He stood up and threw away the Brissago he'd just lit with an expression of disgust. It tasted of straw and glue.

When he reached the road, he walked along for a short way, then turned round and went back past Graf's bicycle shop, looking, looking.

Krock's red sports car had disappeared!

Perhaps it had been put in the garage? – The garage was empty. In the barn? – No. He climbed the steps to the hotel entrance, but the door was bolted, so he went round the building and found the unlocked back door. Inside, he stopped and listened. Not a sound. He took off his boots and set off up the stairs, slowly, taking care not to make any noise.

His Childhood Sweetheart

On the landing between the ground floor and the first floor Studer stopped to listen again. He thought he'd heard a door creak.

Then a scream rent the silence. The sergeant dropped his boots. With two steps he was on the first floor.

The sickroom door was wide open and the daylight flooding in through the opened balcony door. Anni was lying across the threshold, a gash in her right arm from elbow to wrist. The wound was bleeding. Studer bent over her motionless form. "Anni!" he cried. There was no reply. Her eyes were closed. Had she fainted?

"What happened?" the sergeant asked.

The sick man raised his hand – the hand that looked like a crustacean with its shell – and pointed at the balcony door.

"There," he whispered. "Out through there."

Two more steps and Studer was leaning over the balustrade. The area in front of the hotel was empty and there was no one to be seen on the road either. The hay had been gathered into rounded stooks on the steep slope going down to the stream. The heaps looked like gigantic tortoises.

Not a soul in sight anywhere. Beside the balcony was a new metal drainpipe linking the gutter with the ground; a heavy wire ran down beside it. The sergeant examined the wall for traces, but the plaster had not been scraped off anywhere.

"Who?" Studer asked as he went back into the room. He avoided looking at Rechsteiner and kept his eyes on the floor, which was covered with a thin, threadbare carpet. There were no traces there either, not even drops of blood.

Pulling a towel off the rail, the sergeant kneeled down beside the unconscious woman. First he examined the wound. It wasn't deep, not a cut; it looked more as if Anni had caught her arm on a sharp nail and – but that was nonsense. You could catch your clothes on a nail and there would be a tear in the material. But skin wasn't a piece of cloth. No artery had been torn, thank God, nor one of the larger veins. The wound was on the outside of her arm, not on the inside, where the artery ran close to the skin at the wrist. Studer wrapped the towel round Anni's arm, tore his handkerchief into strips and used them to fasten the temporary dressing. Then he picked her up and carried her over to her bed, surprised that the unaccustomed exertion hadn't made him even more breathless.

He sat on the side of the bed and held her wrist in his fingers. Her pulse was regular and very slow. Studer looked at his watch as he counted. He counted quietly, almost with his lips closed, but the hairs of his bushy moustache quivered. He checked her pulse thoroughly, keeping hold of her hand for three minutes; and he did not let go when he put his watch back in his waistcoat pocket. Forty-five to fifty – that was slow, very slow. A case in a village outside Bern came back to mind. A man had tried to commit suicide by swallowing twenty strong sleeping pills. The man's pulse had been just as slow and weak as Anni's . . .

He looked round her bedroom. The shutters on the only window were closed, but there was enough brightness from the light of dawn outside. How pale Anni was! Occasionally her eyelids twitched, but her body was rigid and motionless, like a corpse. Short, shallow breaths. A camphor injection, Studer thought; that was what was needed. But it was only five o'clock in the morning; could one ring Dr Salvisberg that early?

Absent-mindedly the sergeant opened the drawer of the bedside table – and gave a low whistle. A whole box of ampoules! Oil of camphor! And the syringe was beside it. There was even a little phial of ether and some cotton wool.

Studer went about it in a professional manner, cleaned a space on her left upper arm with a swab of cotton wool, sterilized the needle over a lighted match, then filled the syringe with the pungent oil . . .

Five minutes later Anni's chest was rising and falling in deep, regular breaths. For a while Studer stood beside his childhood sweetheart shaking his head. Had she been trying to commit suicide? And if so, why?

He thought back to the previous evening. Anni had been quite reassured by the time they'd gone back to the hotel, hadn't she? True, Martha Loppacher had still been playing at being Rechsteiner's secretary, but that was nothing new. Anni had put up with that for three weeks or more; why should she suddenly decide to kill herself? Studer could see no reason. Though the previous morning she had told the doctor she'd taken a little of her husband's sleeping draught. Pity he hadn't asked what the medicine was.

Restless, the sergeant walked round and round in the room, opened the wardrobe door – dresses, coats, blouses and underwear. But the coats and dresses were old and worn, the blouses and underwear (Studer picked up a few items) patched and mended. It all looked so shabby, so poverty-stricken. Otti, the waitress, was sure to have nicer clothes, more elegant underwear than her employer.

Herbs Good and Bad: A Practical Guide to Medicinal Herbs by Johann Künzle, Herb Pastor in Zizers, near Chur (Switzerland).

770th thousand.

Studer read what was on the green cover of the pamphlet on the bedside table, beside the comb and brush. The comb was old too, a few teeth were missing, and the hairbrush had lost a lot of its bristles.

When was Anni going to wake up? The sergeant went back to the bed – how pale she looked! He'd pulled the clothes right up to her chin because her feet had felt cold.

Should he open the shutters? It turned out to be quite difficult; the wood had swollen and the bolt was stuck. It looked as if they hadn't been opened for ages. Eventually they did open, with a reluctant creak, and slammed back against the outside wall. A leaden sun shone down into the room.

Surely there was a storm brewing. No birds were to be heard. In the distance the clouds were gathering and the wind came galloping along the road, swirling up the dust. Then it suddenly swung round, coming straight at the hotel, took a great leap and was in the room, tearing at the curtains, blowing dust in the sergeant's eyes, leafing

97

through the "practical guide to medicinal herbs" that was still on the bedside table, blowing a sheet of paper stuck in it onto the floor. It toyed with the piece of paper for a while, then jumped back out of the window. Studer watched it rush off down the road.

He rubbed his eyes – the dust was smarting. Then he bent down and picked up the piece of paper that had been hidden in *Herbs Good and Bad.*

Dr Joachim Krock
Legal Advice
Information Bureau
Commission Agents for Loans
65, Bahnhofstr. Tel. 3748

Frau Anni Rechsteiner-Ibach
Schwarzenstein
St Gallen 20th June 19**

In reply to yr esteemed enquiry of 16. 4. we have great pleasure in informing you that we have succeeded in securing a loan of SFr 2,000 on the shares entrusted to us for disposal. We most humbly request that you let us know if we should send you the whole sum by postal order. If you are willing to wait until next Saturday our Herr Jean

Stieger will be in the area on business and will be able to hand over the sum to you personally. We would ask you to inform us of your decision by telephone. We remain

Your obedient servant
(stamp, signature)

Studer folded the letter slowly, very slowly, and put it in his pocket. He went over to the bed and stood there, arms akimbo, for a long time, his eyes fixed questioningly on the woman's pale face.

Two days ago, the day he had been murdered, Jean Stieger had been carrying two thousand francs. Had he handed the money over to Anni? Studer's deduction was that he hadn't, otherwise why would Anni have been having such a heated discussion with Krock immediately after the latter had arrived?

A pity Anni hadn't woken up. He had so many questions to ask her – and there was some reason to hope that this time his questions would be answered truthfully. The sergeant gave a little smile of embarrassment, for he realized that he had not arranged the rendezvous on the bench under the lime tree the previous evening simply in order to renew an old acquaintance and to comfort his childhood sweetheart; it had also been a diplomatic move. He wanted to gain an ally whom he could trust. He wondered whether he had achieved that, but he couldn't be sure until Anni woke up.

Very gently he closed the drawer of the bedside table. As he cast a last glance at the box with the ampoules of camphor oil, he was trying to solve another puzzle. Why did Anni Rechsteiner have this medicament, which was only used in emergencies, so conveniently to hand beside her bed? And together with all the bits and pieces needed for a quick injection: ether, cotton wool, syringe?

There was a simple answer. There was a sick man in the neighbouring room and it was a well-known fact that in the last stages of tuberculosis the heart can often stop. But . . . All the other medicines were on Rechsteiner's bedside table. All with the exception of this one. Did it not then look as if Anni kept the camphor oil for herself? Did she have a heart condition?

Or . . .

Or had she expected what had happened that morning to happen?

It was a nuisance that she was still asleep. Sergeant Studer decided to go down to the kitchen and order himself a very strong black coffee. But there was one thing he felt uncomfortable about. He couldn't bring himself to go through the sickroom with Rechsteiner in it. Was there no other way out of Anni's bedroom? Strangely enough, that room also had a concealed door. It wasn't easy to see, as it had no handle, just a key in the lock. Studer turned the key; the door opened. When he tried to shut it, outside in the darkness of the corridor, he realized there was no handle on the outside either. And it closed so neatly that the gap was invisible in the brown paint covering the walls. But it only needed a gentle push for the door to swing silently open. A strange door.

Suddenly the sergeant was overcome with tiredness after his sleepless night. His legs felt heavy as he went down the stairs, his eyes were smarting and his head was muzzy. He came across the waitress, Ottilia Buffatto, on the steps down to the kitchen.

"Get some strong coffee made," Studer growled, "and take it up to Frau Rechsteiner. She's ill. And if the police come" – the sergeant's speech was becoming blurred with tiredness – "tell them the landlady's ill. And you can tell them I've left. I'm off to bed." He gave such a huge, satisfying yawn his jaws cracked and then – without waiting for an answer; the waitress had nodded, which was answer enough for him – trudged up the stairs to the first floor. He vaguely wondered what the examining magistrate would say about Martha Loppacher and the brother of the bicycle dealer living in the same house. Would the gentleman and his minions assume they were cohabiting? Well, let them, if it amused them. Sergeant Studer was tired, he wanted to sleep, just sleep. He was getting on a bit, over fifty now, not a young thing like Albert.

Albert? His son-in-law? What had he been doing all night? Since he was outside his door, the door with a black "8" on a white background, he might as well ask. He opened the door – it was unlocked. The shutters were closed, but the room was still filled with the summery buzz of flies. From the pillows of one of the beds (hadn't Hedy, the sergeant's wife, been sleeping in it not that long ago?) a head shot up, tousled blond hair.

"Of course," said Studer in a thick voice, "if there's one thing you young folk can do, it's sleep. While older people are hard at it the whole night through. Up you get." Studer found himself singing, "Rise from your sleep, my Switzerland," until he suddenly remembered the dead body in the room next door. He stopped, tossed his jacket onto a chair, one boot in one corner, one boot the other, sank down on the bed, gave a heart-rending yawn and issued his orders sleepily.

Albert was to keep in the background, and watch what the police and the examining magistrate did. "You can wake me at two," the sergeant said, "The worst'll be over by then. And check on Frau Rechsteiner, she's ill. Tell the examining magistrate and his minions to leave her in peace. Understood?"

"Yes," his son-in-law replied. He got up and had a wash.

"Throw me that towel," Studer said, his eyes already closed. "Those bloody flies are a pest." When Albert had complied with this command, he wrapped the towel round his head – and suddenly he was asleep. Albert tiptoed out of the door.

Studer's Dream and Albert's Report

Flies buzzing, buzzing – then two wasps fly in through the heart-shaped holes in the shutters, but the noise their wings make, whirring at furious speed, is quite different from the good-natured drone of the flies. It sounds like a factory siren going off in the distance.

Studer's asleep. Now and then he lifts up his hand and shakes it, because the flies' feet tickle. Then he groans like a soul in torment.

A map, coloured. The glaciers white, the lakes blue. Two particularly large lakes, one in the west, one in the east. But there are other colours on the map. Patches of blue, green, red, purple and brown, each sharply set off from the other. There is a large brown patch almost in the middle – Studer's proud of that one; it's the Canton of Bern, his home.

Studer's crawling round on the map, he's a big fly, with lots of legs. Other flies are crawling all round him, the only odd thing is that they're coloured. Their colours match the separate patches on the map. Then Studer takes off – now he's hovering over the map. Map? It's a country, still small, like the relief images you see in exhibitions, with tiny trees and huts and rivers. Strange the way the relief's expanding; now he's really hovering over a proper country, the rivers are flowing, the woods rustling, smoke's coming out of the chimneys of the houses. But what's that? A gigantic spider's web is spreading out over the land. The threads run from the big lake in the east to the other in the west, shimmering in the sun. The web is a regular net, the threads all coming from one point. Strangely enough, that point is not in the middle of the country, but very close to the eastern lake. And the threads are closer together over the land beside the lake, so close that they look like transparent fabric. Actually, when you look more closely, it's not a point, it's a maze of streets and alleys, houses and factories; a station can be made out too. And there, beside the station, is a building standing alone. The spider's squatting on the roof of the building.

The spider! It only has four legs and is a bluish light grey. It lifts up its head, and now it's Herr Joachim Krock. Studer's still a fly buzzing though the air, but he's noticed that he's getting tired. He'd like to rest somewhere, but he knows that if he lands he'll get caught in the threads and wriggle and wriggle until he wriggles himself to death. But there's a place that's clear, a building beside the white ribbon of the road, a sign on it: Hôtel zum Hirschen.

Studer settles on the roof. And it's odd, in the distance he can see one of the threads crossing the countryside, almost like a power line – only the thread's a shimmering white, not dark like a power line.

Studer strolls up and down the roof-ridge, blinking contentedly in the sunlight and behaving just like a fly. He rubs his hands, passes his arms over his ears, wipes his eyes and is happy – in his dream – with himself and with the countryside, happy too that he's outwitted the light-grey spider by the station. But what's this?

Two hairy hands are clutching the gutter. Feeling, moving up. The arms follow – and a head. Suddenly Studer realizes he can't fly away. A fine thread is running across the roof-ridge, his legs are caught in it, he can't free them – his transparent wings are fluttering in desperation, fluttering with a high-pitched, piercing buzz, like flies when they're stuck on the glue of a fly-paper, the fear of death on them.

The spider is climbing up and up. Its hind legs are already on the gutter. Studer looks at the creature's face – its head's missing. The beast has no head! Or, to be more precise – even in dreams you sometimes want to be precise – instead of a head the human spider has a whitish lump that keeps on changing shape. It's coming nearer; in desperation Studer tears at the thread holding him. He pleads with Heaven to free him. There! A flash of lightning, a peal of thunder. At breakneck speed Studer rolls down the steep roof, straight at the spider with the head that keeps changing shape. But as he rolls past, he suddenly recognizes its face, recognizes it without being able to put a name to it. Once more there's a peal of thunder, a long, dull, rumbling roll . . .

* * *

When Studer awoke he was surrounded by darkness. It became a little brighter when he freed his head from the towel. Then he sat up and listened to the rain hammering on the shutters as if it were demanding to be let in.

One o'clock. Where could Albert be? Studer lay back, his hands clasped behind his head, and thought. His head was clear, as if the sleep had dispersed all the fog surrounding the two murders.

Two murders? Why two? Could the local police not assume, for example, that Krock had decided to commit suicide in a sensational manner? The glasses with the vermouth had been on the table – would it not have been possible for the owner of the Information Bureau to put the poison in his glass himself? That still left the box of pills that had disappeared, but couldn't that have just been put away in the wrong place? He knew better, of course, but why couldn't the local police come to that conclusion?

One thing was certain – Studer himself was surprised he was so sure his observation was accurate that he was willing to swear to it, but he was convinced Martha Loppacher had lied to him. Martha Loppacher and Karl Rechsteiner had foreseen that the sergeant would demand to see the letters that had been dictated that evening. So the two of them – it was striking and suspicious how close they were – had fabricated some letters to show to him. That left the question of why the typist had moved into Ernst Graf's house. Into his workshop. There was one obvious possible explanation: something was hidden in the workshop, so well hidden that the local police hadn't found it when they searched the place yesterday. What? And where was it hidden? In his mind's eye the sergeant saw a hand with painted fingernails, the ball of the thumb pressed against the tip of a file. And the screech of steel on steel rang in his ears once more.

The wound in Anni's arm. Didn't it look as if it had been made with a similar weapon to the one stuck in Jean Stieger's back?

And what was the point of all this? Why did Anni need two thousand francs? After all, it was a substantial sum and her husband was to be kept in the dark.

And another thing: had Joachim Krock been to visit the sick man? Studer shrugged his shoulders. It was too early, much too early to get an answer to all these questions. But Detective Sergeant Studer of the Bern police had done the groundwork, and that was the most important part.

And part of the groundwork was the wet rag slapped across his new black trousers, the conversation under the lime tree with his childhood sweetheart and not only the breakfast with Ernst Graf and "Fräulein" Loppacher, but also the hours from midnight to dawn he'd spent partly in the workshop and partly in the bedroom, over in the bicycle dealer's house.

There was a knock at the door, a very soft, shy knock. And just as softly Studer said, "Come in."

Albert had come to make his report. The first thing he did was to open the shutters and close the windows.

A grey day had settled on the windowpanes outside; the monotonous pitter-patter of the raindrops was soothing. Albert sat down on a chair beside his father-in-law's bed and set out on his report. Beforehand, however, he lit a cigarette, which the sergeant noted with disapproval.

The police and the examining magistrate had turned up at ten, as they had the previous day. Their conclusion? That Joachim Krock had committed suicide. The examining magistrate could see no other solution, nor could the chief of police either. There had been talk of releasing Ernst Graf.

Why? Because they had followed in Studer's footsteps and questioned Graf's brother, Fritz. The interrogation had not been without its problems, but Fräulein Loppacher ("Fräulein", Albert said! Modern youth! Taken in by any painted face. Something would have to be done about that. Studer was proud that his daughter only used powder to beautify herself – if he'd known his wife had bought her daughter a lipstick before she got married!) so: Fräulein Loppacher had acted as interpreter and translated Fritz's laborious stutterings into German, with the result that the officials had come to the conclusion that another course of events was at least possible: Joachim Krock had left St Gallen on Saturday evening; with his car he could easily have been in Schwarzenstein by nine. He could have filed the spoke to a point – the when and the how were something with which the learned gentlemen did not concern themselves, and the fact that one of Bruin's hairs had somehow got stuck to it in the process was not impossible. So then Krock stabbed his assistant. Perhaps he knew too much. "Fräulein" Loppacher had hinted at something of the kind. Then Krock had got into his sports car and spent the night in Rorschach, say, or Heiden (that needed to be checked) and turned up in Schwarzenstein early on Sunday morning to be present at the investigation in the course of which Ernst Graf, bicycle-shop owner, was arrested, a fact that Herr Krock had foreseen and informed his office messenger about even before the police had arrived. But his conscience started to make itself felt. When he went to see the sick man, Rechsteiner, he pocketed the box of pills.

Then he was alone in the dining room, playing the piano. The investigating team had discovered – again from his typist – that Joachim Krock was a music lover. He went to every concert in St Gallen – not the concerts given by the brass band or the local choir, but the ones the posh people went to: string quartets, famous soloists (pianists, violinists); he used to go to Zurich, to Winterthur, even to Paris and sometimes to Germany when there were special si . . . simferny concerts . . .

Studer corrected him: "Symphony concerts. Remember that, Albert. Symphony, that's music with a big orchestra, Beethoven, Schubert, Mozart, lovely stuff . . . but just a minute, Albert."

Studer rolled over onto his side, rested his head on his hand and scrutinized his son-in-law with a pitiless stare. "Now," he said, hesitated and then asked quickly, "what kind of rubbish is that you're smoking? Show me the packet." Albert, somewhat intimidated by the powerful man who even at that moment, lying in bed, sleepy, unwashed and tousled, filled him with great respect, passed over the white packet with his cigarettes. "What?!" said Studer contemptuously. "You smoke this rubbish? Light tobacco? You can't even call it tobacco. It's nothing but straw, perfumed straw. It's all right for apprentices, but men, real men smoke Brissago cigars. Pipes if they prefer. Or at least French cigarettes, they're just about OK. But this rubbish? Yeuch! Here, try one of these."

He produced the slim leather cigar case and instructed his son-in-law in the art of lighting a Brissago. And Albert took a few puffs at it, ten to be precise, before his lips and cheeks went pale and he threw the cigar out of the window.

Studer sighed. Modern youth! A twenty-nine-year-old police corporal and he couldn't take a Brissago. The sergeant pressed a white button and heard a bell tinkle, unreal in the distance. Soon afterwards Otti, the waitress, opened the door and asked why he'd rung.

"Bring that young man there a schnapps," the sergeant said. It was brought, and after he'd drunk it Albert was able to continue his report. But he did not take another cigarette out the whole time. That was what Studer had been aiming for. The smoke from Turkish tobacco gave him a headache.

"So there's Herr Krock, sitting at the piano," the sergeant said.

"Yes," Albert went on, "he's sitting at the piano, the dining room's empty. The waitress comes in with the glasses already filled on a tray, then goes about her business, leaving Krock alone in the room. He gets up, takes a sip of vermouth, drops the pills into his glass, goes back to the piano and continues playing. Then we come in, you and me, Father. Herr Krock clinks glasses with us – he must have been a cool customer – and empties his glass, the poison having dissolved by then, eats his dinner and goes back to the piano. He committed suicide before our very eyes. At least that's their theory."

"Hmm," said Studer, "it wouldn't be such a bad theory – if I hadn't swapped glasses with Krock."

"You, Father? But why?"

Studer shrugged his shoulders. Why? He didn't like the idea of the glasses being already filled, he explained. A new fashion. If you were to be served an appetizer before the meal, an *apéritif* as our French neighbours said, then the custom was to bring the bottle and fill the glasses in front of the guests. But just putting the glasses beside the plates? It wasn't done. He could tell that Albert hadn't been around in the world much, or he would have known a bit more about things. There was one thing he should remember: "Beware of a drink that has not been poured in your presence." And Sergeant Studer raised his forefinger and wagged it slowly and sagaciously.

"But doesn't that mean . . . doesn't that mean . . . that you actually committed the murder?"

"Not a bit of it," the sergeant reassured him. "Anyway, as far I can see, Krock wasn't exactly a pillar of society, not what you'd call a model citizen. Did the police find out anything about him?"

He hadn't managed to hear that, Albert said; the chief of police and the examining magistrate had whispered. The only word he'd been able to make out was "usury".

"Nothing else? Think back carefully."

"Oh, well, yes, now you mention it, there was something else, but I didn't really understand and it didn't seem relevant. It sounded like 'a concert' only it had a funny bit tacked on the end. Do you think Krock was going to perform on the piano somewhere?"

"That's hardly likely. This 'funny bit on the end', what was that like?"

"I don't really know. I had the feeling it might be Latin or Greek, but we never did any of that stuff at school."

"Aha. Could the word perhaps have been 'consortium'?"

"That's it, 'a concertyum'. What's that?"

"An association," said Studer, "but not the kind of association ordinary people like you or me would join. Not with our measly three or five hundred francs a month. High finance. People with" – Studer rubbed his finger and thumb together – "that kind of money."

"Hmm," said Albert, impressed. And actually, that was all that Studer wanted. Who can blame him? Don't we all need the admiration of those around us as much as we need our daily bread? Even if it's only a four-year-old child, or a dog or a cat?

Groaning, Studer got up. At least the Hôtel zum Hirschen was modern enough to have hot and cold running water. It was a convenience. Sergeant Studer could shave in comfort.

A few more guests had turned up at the hotel, Albert told him. And they hadn't turned round and fled when they'd heard of the murder.

Studer, his lips covered in lather, which didn't make speaking any easier, asked whether Krock's car had been found.

Albert was surprised. "Why, has it disappeared?"

"It certainly has," said Studer with a pitying glance at his twenty-nine-year-old son-in-law. Still, one could always hope. He and his wife had brought up their daughter properly and she was an intelligent girl, the man could learn a lot from her. But it was good that Studer had had the chance to work on his son-in-law first.

The rain had stopped and Studer opened the window. There was the roar of a car in the distance. From the noise it must have a pretty powerful engine.

As he rinsed his razor, Studer said, "A consortium of loan sharks. Makes sense. There might be something behind it."

The car was quite close now. It was being driven at full throttle and the occasional misfire could be heard. Studer went to the window and leaned out.

The red sports car! There was a woman at the wheel with a white veil over her hair fluttering in the wind behind her. There was a bright red cross on the band round her forehead. Beside her was a man, but Studer could not tell who he was because he was wrapped up in a grey raincoat with the turned-up collar concealing his face; he also had a cap pulled down low over his forehead.

"Another guest," said Albert. Studer said nothing. The woman, clearly a nurse, got out and hurried up the steps to the hotel. Ottilia appeared at the door, the nurse spoke to her and the waitress went back in, returning with Küng, the groom. Together they lifted the man out of the car and carried him into the hotel, the nurse following with a blanket and a handbag. A suitcase was strapped to the back of the car.

Studer was so involved in observing the scene that the lather dried on his ears with a faint crackling noise. He couldn't take his eyes off the car.

A sports car. Red. The letters for St Gallen on the number plate. There was no doubt at all; the numbers matched too – the car belonged to the late Joachim Krock. And now even Albert had recognized it. "Father," he whispered, "isn't that —"

"Shh," said Sergeant Studer and went to wet his facecloth under the tap. The dried lather was starting to sting. "How's Anni doing?"

"The waitress said she's still asleep. She woke up for a while, long enough to drink the coffee, then went straight back to sleep."

Studer was already on his way out into the corridor, declaring he was hungry. The door to room 7 was open. Ottilia Buffatto and Johannes Küng were putting the new guest in an armchair by the window.

A good thing Studer was holding his son-in-law's arm. A squeeze, a firm squeeze was all that was needed – the lad got the message and kept his mouth shut.

The man in the armchair by the window had taken his cap off and put it on the table beside him – right on the blotting paper Studer had subjected to such a close examination the previous evening. A long, pale-cream silk handkerchief was draped from the breast pocket of his blue-grey jacket and there was a solid gold signet ring on his right index finger. Black hair, as thin and soft as silk, flopped over a high, slightly sloping forehead; a narrow nose jutted out of the smooth face, casting its shadow over the thick lips. The chin was odd: both its shape and colour recalled that of a cement brick.

Why had the sergeant gone to such pains to make sure his son-in-law did not cry out in surprise? Because the stranger's face was strikingly similar to that of the late Joachim Krock; so similar, indeed, that the dead man's face looked like a clay model for the stone sculpture of the new arrival.

"Who is it?" Studer asked the Italian waitress on the stairs.

"*Un direttore francese* . . . the director of a bank from Paris. His name is Gardiny, Giacomo – Jacques – Jakob Gardiny."

What was a French bank director doing in Joachim Krock's red sports car?

Since Studer felt at home in the Hôtel zum Hirschen, he simply went down to the kitchen, without asking, where he managed to charm the skinny cook, who was sitting staring gloomily at a pile of green beans, into giving him a plate of ham, butter and bread. He ate his lunch sitting on a corner of the well-scrubbed table. (Why should that table remind him of the other one down in the cellar?) In between bites he chatted with the old cook and discovered that the *Wormet*, as the locals called vermouth, was kept with the crockery in the dining-room cupboard. When he had finished, he sat down for a quarter of an hour and helped her prepare the beans.

This helping hand melted the icy crust of gloom that had enveloped Fräulein Schätti's soul. She thawed and told the sergeant – in strictest confidence, of course – that the Hôtel zum Hirschen was haunted. "*A bah*," said Studer, had she seen the ghost herself? – Not actually seen, no. But she'd heard it! It crept round the corridors, moaning and groaning to itself, up the stairs, down the stairs. It even went up to the attic and once – it must have been a week ago when she'd been working in the kitchen until almost midnight – it came up to the kitchen door. She'd clearly heard it shuffling around, out there on the stairs, but the light had probably driven it away – A pity ghosts were so afraid of the light, Studer said, for himself he'd love to see one. But since Frau Schätti (Studer addressed her as "Frau" and was pleased to observe the old maid's cheeks turn an even deeper red) had such acute hearing, perhaps she could help him. Had she noticed anything that morning? – That morning? She hadn't slept a wink all night and she'd heard everything that had gone on in the hotel. The last two nights! Each night with a dead body in the building! – That's right, said Studer. And had she heard a car starting? – She nodded vigorously – When was it? – At three o' clock.

Studer thought. At three he'd been sitting surrounded by animals in Graf's shack, and Fritz Graf, who could only talk properly in the dark, had told him his story. That would be why the sound hadn't reached him.

"Yes?" he asked, encouragement in his voice.

"At three I heard someone trying to start a car. I know the sound; my brother's got an old banger and sometimes he has to press the starter a dozen times before the engine fires. That's what it was like this morning. My room, up in the attic, looks out onto the road. I got up and looked out. And do you know who I saw? Otti!"

"*A bah!*" said Studer, since nothing better occurred to him, but he still wanted to express interest in the story. "Can Otti drive?"

"Now that's what I asked myself, Sergeant. She was wearing a blue raincoat, a raincoat I know very well. She drove off, and I stayed awake. She slipped back into her room, very quietly, at five."

"You're sure of that?" When Fräulein Schätti remained silent, offended, he assured her he did not doubt the truth of her story, but was she sure it was Otti and not the ghost?

"You are a wag, Sergeant," she said, then blushed again when she realized she'd used the familiar *du*, and apologized. But Studer gave her a reassuring pat on her bony shoulder. "That's all right, don't take it to heart," he said, using the *du* himself. With a wave of the hand he left the kitchen.

The Village

The road had almost dried out, but the roar of the stream from down in the gorge was loud. What surprised Studer most of all was that there were no dung heaps to be seen. The house walls were covered with shingles, rounded at the bottom and painted blue and white. There were wide projecting roofs jutting out like headscarves to protect the gable ends from sun and rain. He noted with disapproval that the village pond, the purpose of which was to provide water if fire should break out, was covered in duckweed. Then came the church, the only stone building in the village, with the manse beside it, and a small shop. Studer thought of the villages around Bern, of one village in particular where he'd had to investigate a case – and ended up with a few broken bones and pleurisy. In that village, he could see it clearly in his mind's eye, there'd been one shop sign after the other, hanging like paintings in an exhibition. And from the open windows had come the prattling, singing, yodelling of the loudspeakers. In this little Appenzell village, however, it was remarkably quiet. One shop and no inn. The Hôtel zum Hirschen would have a bar and that was sufficient.

The post office. Studer went in and asked for a Bern number. It took five minutes to make the connection. Hedy, Studer's wife, told him everything was all right. Marie, their daughter, was getting the apartment in Arbon ready and waiting for her husband with some impatience. Would he soon be finished out there in the sticks? There'd already been two calls from police headquarters wanting to know where he was – As far as he knew, Studer growled, he was on holiday – Yes, Hedy said, that was true. But as she understood it, there was something big going on there. Perhaps he ought to give the "Old Man" a ring.

Then a voice interrupted the conversation, telling them their three minutes were up.

"'Bye, Hedy," said Studer.

"*Adieu*," came the response.

The "Old Man", as the cantonal chief of police was called by his subordinates, happened to be in his office when Studer rang a few minutes later.

"Sergeant Studer," he said, asking what had happened; his wife had said he was needed in Bern.

A complicated business, he was told; it really was a pity the sergeant was away, just when they could do with him there. The previous day they'd arrested a shady businessman in Interlaken. It was some newspaper small ads that had brought him to their notice: "Loans – no security required. Interlaken Post Box 39." The man had been apprehended and extensive correspondence found in his office. The deputy governor himself had brought all the files to Bern. Among the documents they had seized were some letters signed "Joachim Krock"; they had been sent from St Gallen. And that morning's edition of the *Bund* had reported the death of Joachim Krock; he had apparently committed suicide in some village called Schwarzenstein. Now he, the chief of police, had heard from Frau Studer that the sergeant happened to be in Schwarzenstein at the moment. What was all this about a suicide?

He couldn't really explain it over the telephone, Studer replied, but suicide or not, the man was dead, as was his assistant. Did he have permission to remain in Schwarzenstein until the case was cleared up?

Permission was graciously granted.

Studer took out his watch. Their conversation had lasted ten minutes, but no voice had broken in to remind them that their three minutes were up. It was always the same. You weren't given time for a quiet talk with your wife, but once the authorities were involved . . .

The sergeant came out of the telephone box. The woman behind the counter was casting curious glances at him as she spoke on the telephone. "Yes, Herr Polizeidirektor,

124

of course, Herr Polizeidirektor . . ." What was the woman doing talking to the "Old Man"? Studer asked how much he had to pay and was informed that she had received instructions that the bill for all the . . . er, hmm, er . . . sergeant's telephone calls was to be sent to police headquarters in St Gallen.

Aha. So his holidays were over and he was on an assignment. OK by him. Studer was silent for a while as he scrutinized the postmistress. She didn't seem to be stupid. And she was young as well. Studer rested his forearms on the counter preparatory to a little chat.

He didn't want to push himself forward, he said, but he couldn't help noticing that the Fräulein had been told who he was over the telephone, hadn't she?

"Frau," the postmistress corrected him, "Frau Gloor." And yes, the inspector had told her his name and title and asked her to render assistance wherever she could.

"Render assistance," thought Studer, "that's all I need." But aloud he said he was delighted at that and could she then perhaps answer a few questions for him? Had there been a telephone call to the Hôtel zum Hirschen the previous night? – Yes, around two in the morning – Where from? – From Rorschach – And who had replied in the hotel? – The Italian woman – And had Frau Gloor been able to understand what was said?

The postmistress blushed, which suited her. Yesterday, she explained, she had been instructed by the examining magistrate to listen in to calls to and from the hotel. Unfortunately she didn't understand enough Italian – and the woman had been speaking in dialect into the bargain. She was sure the sergeant knew how difficult it was to understand Italian dialects.

Studer nodded.

However, she had been able to pick up a few words: *automobile*, *rosso*, *subito*, *stazione* – Who had been speaking? A man or a woman? – A woman (The nurse, Studer thought.) At two in the morning!

Hm. That was about the time the Paris–Salzburg–Vienna express went through Rorschach. But it was impossible, absolutely impossible, that Jacques Gardiny, the bank director, had come because of the death of Joachim Krock. The owner of the Information Bureau had died at nine o'clock – and the bank director had arrived at two. Why would the man, who was paralysed, make the journey from Paris to a tiny village in Appenzell? He would presumably claim it was for his health. But there must be another reason why he had turned up. Jean Stieger's death? Could this Jean Stieger, whose face bore a look of truly international nastiness, have been the real owner of the business in St Gallen and Krock merely the front man?

Studer was so deeply immersed in his thoughts that he completely forgot to bid farewell to the friendly post-mistress, but her "*Adieu*, Sergeant. Hope I see you again," reminded him of his manners.

"Goodbye. And thank you, Frau Gloor."

Where would be the quietest place to go and think? Where was he least likely to be disturbed? The graveyard. It spread out behind the church and there was a bench against the church wall. Studer sat down. Some of the graves looked like large molehills; others were little flower-beds, such as children make when they're playing at being gardeners. Here and there wreaths were withering, the ribbons on them like faded flags that had fluttered through many a battle. The clouds had withdrawn back across Lake Constance, to Swabia, leaving behind just a few thin, threadbare scraps through which the deep-blue, summery sky could already be seen. But the back of the church faced north and he was quite happy with that, preferring the shade to the sun for the moment. It was quiet, unbelievably quiet. Just now and then there was a sound in the grass like a dwarf hammering on glass and silver – but it was just a cricket or grasshopper.

The dead were well off. They'd put everything behind them: their own wedding, the christenings, their children's weddings. No more detection for them, no more playing at being a mole and digging dark passages underground. They had made their last molehill and were sleeping beneath it, waiting. Were they really waiting? What for?

But such morbid thoughts were, as Sergeant Studer put it, *Chabis*. However, he immediately withdrew the expression. No, they weren't nonsense, such thoughts were all right, they were good thoughts; it was just a pity he couldn't give himself up to them more often. It was a good thing, the lonely man thought, to reflect on death now and then. It helped you to distance yourself from all the hustle and bustle, not to take things too seriously, neither your work, nor yourself. Success and failure looked quite different seen from the perspective of a graveyard.

For example the Stieger/Krock case. Would the thoughts the case gave rise to stand up in the court of the dead? Let's see . . .

Reflections in a Graveyard

The Stieger case: the most unusual thing about the case was the murder weapon. Just a minute, that wasn't quite right. In itself the spoke from a bicycle wheel was no more unusual than a hatpin, a knitting needle or a rapier. Did it not look as if the murderer – leaving aside for the moment the question of who the murderer might be – were deliberately trying to send a message to the police? If a hatpin had been used, their immediate assumption would have been that the murderer was a woman. A rapier would have suggested a fencer. And a steel spoke from a bicycle wheel – a man who sold bicycles. One lived nearby; a witness (Johannes Küng) had seen him hanging round the hotel. Moreover the man from the bicycle shop possessed a dog and a hair from that dog had been stuck to the spoke. So the police had been quite correct in arresting Ernst Graf, the "reg'lar buck", on the basis of that circumstantial evidence, as the expression was. Especially when you added the fact that the said bicycle dealer was in love with a painted "Fräulein" who had thrown herself on the dead body like a character from a film with the words, "My beloved!"

But: Jean Stieger looked like nastiness incarnate. Just a minute! That was the personal, purely subjective impression of a fifty-year-old detective sergeant from Bern. A detective sergeant wasn't infallible. It could easily be that the sudden attack had caused his features to contort and his ensuing death had left that expression on his face. That was one possibility. On the other hand, there were two little incidents the above-mentioned detective from Bern happened to have observed, but which until then had remained hidden somewhere inside his brain. Now they suddenly emerged into the light.

Studer ran the two incidents through his mind: the wedding party's sitting at a table in the dining room. No one has much of an appetite because the lunch has been more than ample. At half past eight the waitress brings the coffee. Hedy pours it. At that point a man, very tall, certainly over six foot, comes into the room. He sits at the table by the door and the waitress brings him a tall glass a quarter full with some foreign spirits. As she places a soda siphon on the table, he puts his arm round her waist; she pulls away and goes out. The man stays there, slowly drinking his whisky. The clock over the dining-room door says a quarter to nine. The young man gets up and leaves. Three minutes later the detective sergeant from Bern gets up as well; it's too close in the room, even though the windows are open; he'd like a breath of unadulterated fresh air. The door leads into a corridor running along the rear wall of the hotel. At the end is a door. Studer pushes it open. It's dark outside, there's just a faint light from the corridor windows. The sergeant takes a few steps, then he hears hissing, a groan, little cries of anger. Cats fighting? No. The whisky drinker is holding the waitress and trying to kiss her. The girl's resisting, desperately trying to fight him off. Immediately the sergeant is beside the struggling pair. Whenever there's a brawl, the spectators get worked up as well. The sergeant's just wondering whether to give the young lout a clip round the ear, already his fists are clenched, when the lad lets the girl go, puts his hands in his trouser pockets – that's right, he's not wearing a jacket and his shirt has short sleeves – and strolls off, whistling.

"Did he hurt you, Fräulein?" Studer enquires. A shake of the head. But the look in her eyes! Fury and hatred. Perhaps . . . perhaps the wet floor cloth was slapped round the trousers of his Sunday suit the next morning simply because he had chanced to observe that fury and that hatred.

The second incident, the same evening: half an hour later, a quarter past nine by the dining-room clock. The landlady comes in. She pays no attention to the young man by the door, but comes straight over to the table with the wedding party, asks if everything is all right, tells them she has ordered the horses to be fed. If it's fine by them, the carriages will be ready at half past ten. It'll be a lovely night ride; they'll be in Arbon by midnight at the latest. But, she adds with a smile, the newlyweds must have a carriage to themselves. Albert blushes, Marie blushes, Hedy laughs and all the aunts and cousins join in. Someone shouts the comment to Frau Guhl, who's hard of hearing. Studer, however, is thinking how tired Anni looks, how sad and apprehensive. And he quietly asks his childhood sweetheart if Rechsteiner's worse again. A silent shake of the head. Then she says goodbye to everyone, goes to the door, sees the man – and clutches at her heart. Why? Does she have a heart condition? Studer sees the man's impudent grin quite clearly. Anni goes to his table and asks a quiet question. The man shakes his head; his grin is gloating now. Then he whispers something, tapping the table with his forefinger. It looks as if he's making conditions. Anni shakes her head. Studer watches her lips and manages to read them: "I can't do that." Then a third person appears on the scene – the table over there really does look as if it's in a stage set – a young woman in a white dress, the neck and hem trimmed with fur. She stands in the doorway looking at the two of them. Anni seems to sense her look, for she turns round. What does the girl want? From his place at the table Studer can't see her face, but from Anni's reaction it is clear that the woman in white looks angry. Anni leaves without a word. She has to push past the young woman in the door, since she refuses to make way for her. Then the man says out loud – everyone in the room can hear it – "*Salut*, Martheli, you little . . ." An obscene word. Frau Studer has heard it and the sergeant too. They both start to talk in loud voices, while the woman in the fur-trimmed dress sits down at the man's table and empties his glass, as if it were the most natural thing in the world. The two whisper. The woman gets up, beckons to the man, who follows her. Automatically the sergeant looks at the clock: half past nine.

How long does it take to file a spoke to a point? Five minutes if you have a vice. And the vice over there in the bicycle workshop isn't the only one; the groom, Johannes Küng, has one too. It goes back to the time when Rechsteiner was still well and used to do all the repairs in the hotel himself. Anni had told the police that the day after the murder.

Anni, Martha Loppacher and Ottilia. There was the possibility that one of those women had committed the murder. They all had a motive.

Anni to start with. Childhood sweetheart or no, personal feelings had no place in the court of the dead. Only facts counted for the dead. They were objective, impersonal; they never took sides. The dead were impartiality itself. While all the living – assuming they were truly alive and not just living dead, stumbling through the world like Egyptian mummies – had to take sides . . . Strange, the thoughts that came to you in a graveyard.

So, to start with Anni: there was the letter in which she tried to raise a loan on her shares. Jean Stieger was supposed to bring the money. On the day of the wedding – how long ago that now seemed! – he hadn't been able to make sense of their little mime show. But now, after he'd seen the letter hidden in Pastor Künzle's herbal, he could at least attempt an interpretation.

Anni asks: "Have you come from St Gallen? Have you got the money?" The question is put in such anxious tones that the man, whose one satisfaction is to make others feel his power, that Jean Stieger feels impelled to torment the woman. Perhaps he says that he can't deliver the money (didn't he shake his head?) without her husband's prior consent. Perhaps he goes on to say (didn't he tap the table with his finger?) that they could come to an agreement. "Give your waitress the day off tomorrow, I want to go out with her, go dancing, and you can have your money tomorrow evening, before I leave." And Anni replies, "I can't do that" (the words he read from her lips). Then

Martha Loppacher interrupts the conversation, with the result that Jean Stieger calls her such a foul name that two people at the wedding table start to talk loudly to cover it up.

But Anni Rechsteiner needs the money. Not the next evening, no, she needs it that very day, Saturday. Why? "Rechsteiner has ordered Ottilia to keep me under surveillance. His own wife! Every Saturday evening the waitress has to go to his bedside with all the week's bills and receipts, and I have to stand there and listen to his criticisms: this was wrong and that was wrong and why hadn't I charged that guest more? Then Rechsteiner adds up the takings and sends me out." When had Anni told him that? The previous evening. Perhaps a sum has been missing for a long time? So far she's managed to conceal it, but today everything has to add up. She has to have those two thousand francs. What would a woman not do if she were driven to despair? So it was Anni, then?

"Fräulein" Loppacher? The only motive he could find was the name Stieger had called her. Anything else? Yes. Why had she put a blunt nail in the vice the previous evening and started to file away at it? And not without a certain skill.

But too many things spoke against it. It was impossible that the murderer's clothes should not be bloodstained.

Now Fräulein Loppacher had thrown herself over the dead body – no, just a minute, that wasn't right. She had gone down on her knees *beside* the body, but then Albert had pulled her back with a curt "don't touch".

And Studer had been present the previous day, when the local police had searched her room. Everything had been there: the fur-trimmed dress, the white stockings, the light-coloured shoes, but there had been no trace of blood on any of them. Studer had checked himself to make sure.

But why had the typist been in such a hurry to move into the bicycle workshop? Why? The two of them were in love. Was that a valid reason, to use the jargon, for the move? Studer had heard Ernst Graf, before he was led away, whisper to her, "Look after my animals." And she had done his bidding, had left her elegant hotel room for the dusty workshop and was staying there, with no modern conveniences, no running water, no bathroom, no make-up and powder. But had the animals been the only reason for the move? Was there another?

Studer leaned back on the bench. The clouds were advancing for another assault on Lake Constance. The sky was turning grey; a strong, patient wind was starting to blow again, stroking the tips of the grass with its huge hand, making them bow before it. There was a white steamer on the lake, tiny as a toy boat, smoke coming out of its funnel like tangled grey whorls of metal, off-cuts from a lathe . . .

A thread had been cut into the blunt end of the spoke. What was the purpose of the spiral? To screw a handle on. And where was the handle? Perhaps Martha Loppacher had abandoned her comfortable room in the Hôtel zum Hirschen in order to look for the hidden handle in the workshop? But . . . but that meant Ernst Graf was the guilty man? Or, to put it more precisely: that meant Martha Loppacher *thought* Ernst was the guilty man.

A handle. Easy to hide. The police had organized a search of the premises, of course. It had been fruitless. So fruitless that they were already talking of releasing Graf because it was within the bounds of possibility that Joachim Krock had committed the murder.

Joachim Krock. He had come to Schwarzenstein, played the piano, spoken to the police, argued with Anni, drunk a glass of *Wormet* and died. And a banker from Paris, by the name of Gardiny, had told the Italian waitress to drive the dead man's car to Rorschach, had arrived at the hotel that afternoon and demanded the room where Joachim Krock, owner of an information bureau in St Gallen, had stayed . . .

A case of duplication, as the jargon had it: Martha

Loppacher had moved into the bicycle workshop to look for something and Gardiny had demanded the room of Krock, the – not to put too fine a point on it – loan shark. Probably in the hope of finding something in the room, something the local police and a detective sergeant from Bern had missed. There was no doubt about one thing: the gang or – to use a less damning word – the associates must have been well aware of the sergeant's reputation. That was the only explanation for the poisoned vermouth.

Studer could visualize the scene in the dining room clearly and he remembered the thoughts that had gone through his mind. After all, it had only been the previous evening. Nobody had paid any attention to him when he had swapped the glasses round. And even now he couldn't give a full reason why he'd done it. He was suspicious of glasses that were already filled; that was all. And his suspicion had cost a man his life. But charity began at home, they said. However inviting the molehills before him were, promising rest and peace, the sergeant had no desire to shuffle off his mortal coil just yet. So he had swapped the glasses round, unsuspecting.

But there was one thing he could swear to: neither Joachim Krock, nor the waitress, nor he himself had known that the vermouth in one of the glasses had been poisoned.

"*Prost.*" – "Your health." – "Cheers." Krock drinks, then puts his glass down. No searching glance at the sergeant. However much a man has himself under control, he would find it impossible to repress a twitch of the facial muscles, a flutter of the eyelids, a look in the eyes. And even if he had managed to keep all those reactions under control, there would at least be a quaver in his voice.

Nothing! Nothing! And nothing like that from Otti either. And Anni? That very same evening he'd been sitting under the lime tree with his childhood sweetheart. Anni had been sad, had complained about Rechsteiner, but that was all.

Now don't get ahead of yourself. Take each thing in turn. And presumably the dead won't have any objection if you light up a Brissago to help you concentrate . . .

So: the atropine/hyoscine pills – the medicine made from deadly nightshade and henbane – were on Rechsteiner's bedside table. Who had been in the room? Fritz Graf, after his brother had been arrested, Martha Loppacher, Anni, Ottilia, the doctor, Joachim Krock. If the poison really was Rechsteiner's medicine for night sweat, then one of those six must be the guilty person. One of them must have wanted to get the sergeant out of the way. Rechsteiner didn't count: he was paralysed.

Actually, it was a bit odd when you thought about it,

Rechsteiner's being paralysed. Studer vaguely remembered that the final stages of consumption were accompanied by great weakness – but paralysis? However, Rechsteiner was paralysed. Anni had said so and Dr Salvisberg had confirmed it.

Of the six people who had gone to see the sick man, four could be excluded: the doctor, Otti, Anni and Joachim Krock.

"Go on, grin in your graves," Studer muttered. He had the feeling the dead were making fun of him. So he addressed them, the ones who stuck to the facts, who didn't take sides. "I know ruling out those four is only based on feeling. Only based on feeling? Well, not quite. Expressions observed on people's faces, those are facts, aren't they? So it's on the basis of those facts that I rule out those four. And a similar fact leads me to rule out a fifth: Graf's brother. His face was brightly lit by the lamp above the workbench and the expression on it was that of a man in torment. A man who can't speak, only stammer, because his father beat him so much the fear's become part of him. Why should Fritz have wanted to kill me? He didn't know me. He could have been told I think Ernst is innocent. I'm sure he was told. Would that man then go and put poison in my vermouth? No one saw him creeping into the dining room either. Therefore? . . .

"Which leaves Martha Loppacher. Joachim Krock had called his typist a silly goose. Perhaps I've underestimated the girl? Perhaps she's wilier than I thought. She could go into the dining room without attracting attention, poison the *Wormet*, then slip away again. Just a minute, there's another point against her. She's been here on full board for a month: that means she's been in the dining room for breakfast, lunch and dinner. She knows where the spirits are kept. And yesterday of all days was the one time she didn't turn up. Where did she have her dinner? With Fritz Graf?"

Studer shook his head. And yet, and yet . . . Something didn't add up. Even if all the circumstantial evidence pointed to the Loppacher woman, the logical conclusion creaked like two pieces of metal that didn't quite fit. A shaft in a bore, for example; the shaft turns, but it's a hundredth (perhaps even less) of an inch too small and the engine doesn't run properly, eventually dies.

In the first place there were the empty envelopes in Jean Stieger's back pocket. What point was there in taking the letters and leaving the envelopes? Just a minute. Didn't that come in the same category as the bicycle spoke and the dog hair? They had been used to shift suspicion onto the bicycle dealer. That was fairly certain. Now what if the murderer had left the envelopes there in order to give whoever was investigating the case a little nudge? "Look, every other day Martha Loppacher's written to St Gallen. Don't you think that's a bit suspicious? You don't write that often when you're on holiday. Even if you're a woman and in love. And long letters. Business letters? Must be a shady business."

Someone had slipped into the hotel cellar between midnight and four o'clock in the morning to take the letters. According to Fräulein Loppacher, they were just carbons of the letters Rechsteiner had dictated to her. Of course, the woman could just as well have been lying.

He had to start putting his facts together. For example, the cook had said the hotel was haunted. A ghost crept round at night, from the cellar to the attic, groaning. Even if, as a rational detective, he didn't believe in ghosts, that was no reason to dismiss the cook's statement out of hand. Seen in a different light, it meant that a stranger was creeping round the hotel, looking for something, looking for it at night. So that meant it was this stranger who had taken the letters. Therefore they must contain dangerous information. A stranger couldn't stay in the hotel without an accomplice. He must at least have a man to help him. Why a man? Could it not just as well be a woman?

Who were the candidates? Only one. Ottilia. Ottilia Buffatto. He'd not paid much attention to her, and yet she seemed to play a leading role. Was it usual for a waitress to know how to drive a car? Was it usual for a waitress, and a foreigner into the bargain, to be taken into a man's confidence more than his lawful wedded wife? How was it that a banker from Paris, and a cripple as well, had rung a servant in an unknown hotel in the middle of the night and the servant had taken an abandoned car, driven to Rorschach and then come back on foot? How was it that this Eyetie girl had connections with international high finance?

Studer knew Paris inside out and the name Gardiny was familiar to him. There was a whole host of myths attached to the name. He had amalgamated a Dutch, a French and a Belgian bank, financed the rebuilding of areas destroyed in the war, set off inflation in Germany and then stopped it, finally arranged credits for several German cities, especially German cities that had been occupied by France after the war: Ludwigshafen, Mannheim . . .

Mannheim!

Who was it Joachim Krock had been writing to on the afternoon prior to his death? The Mannheim chief of police.

Where had Rechsteiner earned his money?

Mannheim.

What had he managed to decipher from the blotting paper (apart from the name of the town)?

"Forged cheque". A number: "30,000" or "50,000". And a year, the last digit of which was unclear, a 4 or a 7 – couldn't it also have been a 1?

It was ten years ago that Rechsteiner had married Anni Ibach. Ten years ago – 1921. That was when the inflation in Germany had started. At that time a Swiss franc was worth twenty marks. Later the German currency had climbed to billions. No, climbed wasn't the right word; it had been a fall, a plunge into a bottomless pit. And three years ago Rechsteiner had gone to a health resort in the South Tyrol. Why to the South Tyrol? Wasn't there Leysin in Switzerland, and Davos and Arosa, places where the tuberculosis clinics were as thick on the ground as the stalls at Basel Fair? Why had Rechsteiner not gone to a Swiss health resort? No, he had to go to the South Tyrol, to Italy. And alone! He had a good excuse for going alone – his wife had to run the hotel while he was away.

"All a lie!" the sergeant said out loud, thinking of the letters Martha Loppacher had shown him. "A stinking lie!" Rechsteiner didn't need a thousand, two thousand, three thousand francs. The letters were faked. Faked to mislead a detective from Bern.

Strange how the landlord of the Hôtel zum Hirschen, a sick man whose asymmetrical face with its yellowish complexion recalled the waning moon, how this man was suddenly taking centre stage in the investigation. The sergeant was reminded of his dream, the dream of the spider sitting on a building beside St Gallen station, the threads of its web stretching across the land, white glittering threads, sticky too, in which the human flies get caught, then wriggle and buzz. But they can't free themselves. The spider creeps up on them and sucks their blood dry: innkeepers, small farmers, tradesmen, office workers. They're still too decent and honest; they were brought up to believe it's dishonourable not to pay your debts. That's why there are others who profit from these ordinary people's honesty. But if the loans that have been taken up by the cities (Studer was thinking of Mannheim) are suspended, what then? Then they make do with lower profits.

A consortium of usurers. Why shouldn't there be one in these crazy times? In fact, if you really thought about it, the whole business was usury, more or less. Take the loans granted to poor countries, for example; the countries had to mortgage the revenue from their customs dues, from their monopolies. And who – if you looked at it with an open mind – did that mean had to pay the interest on the loans? Ordinary people! *They* needed salt and tobacco and spices and coffee, *they* travelled on the trains, *they* paid the taxes. Of course, it looked as if it were the minister of finance who supplied the money. But in reality the minister – or the burgomaster, if it was a city servicing a loan – bought himself a Buick, if not a Cadillac or a Lincoln, and built himself a fine house outside the city.

Things were a little different in Switzerland, true. Very different? Not really. Studer thought of a member of the government who had had to resign because the butcher, the baker, the candlestick-maker had refused him any more credit. How easy would it be for a respected figure like that to fall into the clutches of – a consortium of usurers.

But enough idle thoughts. Not that the dead would have become impatient because one of the living was laying out his thoughts before them, but time was getting short; he had to come to some kind of conclusion.

The clock on the church tower struck six as Studer threw the chewed-up end of his Brissago over the churchyard wall. Just a few steps and his broad, calm figure was at the post office counter again, demanding two telegram forms. He could see the glint of curiosity in the eyes of the young postmistress and he smiled. He went over to a high desk and took out his wallet, but his broad back was a big enough screen to conceal what he did from female curiosity.

And the sergeant's smile was even broader as he passed the two telegrams over the counter. The addresses were

146

perfectly understandable: "Police Headquarters, Mann-heim" and "Madelin, *Police judiciaire*, Paris", but the follow-ing letters and words brought a look of baffled disap-pointment to the young woman's face:

"Wrdasi ptamtschicky wontzürabei igbalsgar yolutzi-brasch."

"What's that?" she asked.

"Polcod," Studer replied, shrugging his powerful shoulders. "You don't know what Polcod is? Police code, our international code. To keep our secrets from prying eyes. And get the telegrams off immediately. Top priority, yes? Reply paid. And you can send the bill to St Gallen. *Adieu.*"

The Village (part two)

As Studer came out of the post office, he saw a man coming towards him whose profession was so clear from his whole manner and dress that it would have been a waste of time asking him what he did. A black frock coat came down to his knees, his waistcoat left just a tiny triangle of starched shirt visible, below the turned-up points of his collar was a little black bow tie that was held in place by an elastic band round his neck. A moustache similar to the sergeant's covered his mouth when he was silent, and when he spoke his lower lip freed itself from the bristly curtain and revealed itself as thin, red and mobile.

"Ah, a very good day to you, Sergeant," said the man in black. Familiar sounds! What was a Bernese pastor doing in an Appenzell village?

"Good day to you, Pastor," Studer replied, slipping into his home dialect as he shook the man by the hand. It was dry, bony and warm.

"Found anything today?" Herr de Quervain asked after he had introduced himself.

"Nothing special," Studer said. Just the man he needed!

148

The pastor would surely know everything that was going on in the village.

They walked down the street together. The little windows, which took in the whole of the façade of the houses, were curtained – but the curtains were moving. There was no doubt about it: the detective from Bern had aroused the locals' curiosity. Even if it were only old women lurking behind the curtains, old women have agile tongues. The presence of the sergeant and his conversation with the pastor were sure to be discussed round the dinner table. Studer immediately took advantage of Herr de Quervain's invitation to visit some of his flock. He had decided not to return to the hotel until after dark, and there was time to fill until then.

Houses, houses, houses – and all the same. Four, sometimes five steps up to the front door, then a kind of vestibule where, the pastor explained, they took their meals in the summer. From this room a door led into the kitchen and from there one led off at a right angle into the main living room. They were very handsome, these old, wood-panelled rooms with long windows looking out onto the street, windows which were long but not high and fitted into the wood of the walls without hinges. Two or three could be opened, that is, slid up. There were flowerpots in front of them: geraniums glowing red and, as if their own colour were not enough, soaking up the crimson rays of the setting sun.

Herr de Quervain did his best to allay the suspicion that Studer's appearance always aroused, but it was not too difficult. The sergeant from Bern knew how to strike the right note. He talked about Anni Rechsteiner, who had been his childhood sweetheart, and the effect was remarkable. The landlady's name loosened tongues and dispelled suspicion. The woman of the house or, if she was still out in the fields, the grandmother, immediately relaxed. Oh yes, Anni Rechsteiner. Nothing wrong with her. Decent! Hardworking! If, on the other hand, the sergeant started talking about the landlord of the Hôtel zum Hirschen, lips were suddenly sealed; fear crept into people's eyes, which avoided his and wandered round the nooks and crannies of the room. Then it was better to take their leave. The pastor gave the sign and they departed. Outside he said:

"These people owe money to Rechsteiner too. It's understandable. Farming's never brought in much up here. Their main source of income was embroidery; farming came second. But since the economic crisis, all the embroidery machines have fallen silent. Before that – oh, yes, before that you could hear people singing in all the houses. Sometimes they swore as well; that goes with any honest labour. The man would be sitting at the pantograph, his daughter threading the needles, his wife giving a hand here and there – they could make a living."

They went into another house. The man was at home. His wife was in the kitchen peeling potatoes, which she dropped into a pan, while he was sitting at the table reading the newspaper. There was such a feeling of hopelessness about the room it made Studer shiver.

Things couldn't go on like this, the man said. He was unshaven and his hair, which had not been cut for a long time, hung down over the tops of his ears and his neck. He seemed to become aware of it himself, for he blushed. He didn't even have a franc to spare for the barber, he muttered. And no hope things would get better. Did the pastor think you could support a family – wife, husband and three children – on five acres? And pay interest? To that Rechsteiner? If he could just get his hands on the man, he said, clenching his fist. At first it had sounded as if he had come to help. "See, Hans," he'd said, "I'm a sick man, what use is all this money to me? I know you need it, how much can I give you? Three thousand? You won't get anywhere with that, let's say five. Look, here's the money." And Rechsteiner had waved a bundle of hundred-franc notes. "You'd better sign here. Just so that things are in order, so my wife'll be all right once I'm dead. You don't need to bother reading it. You trust me, don't you?" And he'd signed, said the man, idiot that he was. Then last Saturday this young brat had turned up – not even wearing a jacket, he was – he'd come straight in, bold as brass, without even knocking. The fact was, he said, that Herr Rechsteiner had made over all debts owed him to Krock's Bureau in St Gallen. He was the agent of Herr Joachim Krock and since the gentleman had signed an agreement to pay on 1 July, he was already a month in arrears.

"He showed me the piece of paper – Six thousand it said I owed! Five per cent for payment in arrears and expenses and I don't know what else. So instead of owing five thousand, I owe six thousand three hundred. Where can I get that kind of money? And I signed because I trusted him. You have to trust a man on his deathbed, haven't you, Pastor? What shall I do now? He threatened to have me declared bankrupt, our property auctioned off. I did hear the fellow's since died, but there are others behind him, others I don't know. And our lovely embroidery machine! Come and have a look at it."

The shutters were closed. The pantograph looked like the withered arm of an eighty-year-old. There was dust everywhere, on the machine, which hadn't been oiled for ages, and on the chairs; on the windowsill was a thick layer looking like a piece of rotten cloth and the tiny scraps of embroidery silk were patterns woven in by time, all the time the machine had been lying idle.

"It's the same everywhere," the pastor said once they were outside. "At least Messmer was honest with you, Sergeant. But Rechsteiner's done that to all the men, advanced them money and got them to sign a piece of paper, which they didn't read because they trusted him. But do you think I can get them to institute a joint action for usury? Impossible. Moan, yes, they can do that, but that's all. And they'll pay if they can. They don't want to become the laughing stock of other villages, they say, they'd rather let their houses and farms and fields be distrained and auctioned off. It looks to me as if the men behind this speculation knew exactly what kind of people they were dealing with. It's impossible that Rechsteiner himself raised all the money that's been lent in this village alone. Just think: thirty farms and in each one there's a man who had at least five thousand francs. At least, I say. Some took ten thousand, twenty thousand – one (he has five acres of woodland) even forty thousand. Let's say fifteen thousand on average: thirty times fifteen thousand makes four hundred and fifty thousand, round it up to half a million. It's the same in Grab and in Happenröti and in Rabentobel. I'm not exaggerating when I say that around two million francs have been 'invested' (as the financiers would say) in the area round here."

With that the pastor fell silent.

Studer thought: the spider! So my dream wasn't deluding me after all. How is it that we sometimes see the truth in our dreams? The psychiatrist friend I once helped solve a case in his asylum always used to say the subconscious is much cleverer than the rational mind. But, my friend said, we have to be able to understand the symbolic language of the subconscious, puzzle out its images. Isn't it the case that the spider on the building by the station in St Gallen has thrown out its net over the whole of Appenzell? A profitable speculation! If the state goes bankrupt, nothing much can happen to it – you can't lock up the whole state, that is everyone involved in government. They'd have to arrest themselves. But a single person? In such a case the law operates infallibly, and if not civil law, then criminal law. Bankruptcy with intent to defraud.

"Pastor," Studer said, stopping in the middle of the street. A few scraps of the grey day were still clinging to the tops of the trees, the ridges of the roofs. But night was already gathering up these scattered remnants, which otherwise would have stuck to its blue-black dress, its silken train sweeping along behind; and the evening breeze, coming to meet it, made the silk, with its silver embroidery, billow out. Then the night settled on the western hills, the wind dropped and the shimmering material of the train spread out over the silent countryside.

"Pastor," Studer repeated. His companion could tell that he found it difficult to speak. "I have a request. Could you come to the hotel early tomorrow?"

"Early, Sergeant? What do you call early?"

Studer did not reply. He was working out the time, lips closed. He'd sent off the telegrams at six, which was pretty late; all offices were sure to be closed by then. But in Paris, as Studer knew, there was at least one man on night duty. His telegram would reach the *Police judiciaire* – the criminal investigation department – by seven at the latest; and at half past it would be in the hands of his friend, Commissaire Madelin.

Enquiries – say six hours. Assuming that some could only be made the next day, once the offices were opened, then the answer would arrive in Schwarzenstein by ten at the latest. And things would take a similar time at police headquarters in Mannheim . . .

"What do you call early, Sergeant?" the pastor repeated.

"Let's say half past ten. Can you manage that? Good. Don't ask for me, ask for Anni . . . er . . . Frau Rechsteiner. She'll tell you where to find me."

"And do you think, Sergeant, that you can sort all this

out?" He waved his slim hand in a gesture taking in the whole of Schwarzenstein.

"I think so, Pastor," said Studer in his gruff Bernese.

And if, at that moment, someone had ventured to make a derisive remark or a cheap joke about men of the cloth, he would have found himself spending the rest of the night applying cold compresses to his bruised cheek. Herr de Quervain was all right. It was plain to see that his parishioners' wretched plight had touched him to the heart. He was a small man, hardly coming up to Studer's shoulder, and he looked slightly ridiculous with his black frock coat flapping round his knees, but the way he accepted the sergeant's arrangement, without questioning it or worrying about what the consequences might be, showed he had not lost his trust in his fellow man.

Preparations for the Final Battle

The local authorities, in the shape of one examining magistrate, one chief of police, several detectives and one secretary, had not been too insistent, so the detective from Bern had managed to keep three of the empty envelopes found in the wallet of the late Jean Stieger. With their knowledge. The sergeant did not say what he meant to do with the three envelopes, nor did anyone ask him.

Two blankets have been fixed with strong drawing pins to the window frame. No light can get into the room from outside. There is red paper wrapped round the lamp on the bedside table, but the room is so dark you have to keep your eyes closed for at least three minutes before you can see anything when you open them. The camera is on the table, fully extended, and in front of it, inserted into a printing frame, an envelope with the inside facing the lens. The red light is switched off; the darkness is so thick it's almost tangible. A click: the shutter is open. A flash: magnesium. Now the red light is on again. Develop, fix. The plate is washed in pure alcohol. Albert, his son-in-law, has to operate the bellows Fräulein Schätti the cook had no objection to Sergeant Studer taking. God, it does take ages for a plate to dry! At last! Once more the red light's switched off. The dried plate is inserted back into the printing frame over a highly sensitive one. This time it's just a match that flares up, goes out. Groping fingers unscrew the plates in the all-encompassing darkness; the one underneath is developed, fixed, intensified. The red light can be switched back on during the intensifying process. The same procedure as before: the plate is dipped in alcohol, shaken. Albert is operating the bellows so vigorously the sweat is running down from his forehead. Finally the plate is dry. Now the second plate is inserted in the frame on top of a highly sensitive plate and again a match flares up – after the red light has been switched off, of course. What's the time? Half past twelve. They've been at it since ten. Studer's wristwatch with the luminous dial has been hidden under the pillow. A match flares up another three times – another three times the bellows are blown after the plate has been developed, fixed and intensified. Here's the last plate – and Studer can look on his work with pride – he feels like shouting "Eureka"; he'd even like to copy the philosopher, who ran naked through the streets of Syracuse because he'd discovered gold was lighter in water than in air. Yes, Sergeant Studer would like to run round the meadow behind the hotel and roll in the grass in his birthday suit because, even though he's only got his pyjamas on, he's wet from head to toe.

But now they can take the blankets off the window and let in the night air. It's raining, thank God; fine, cool rain is singing its song in the night, quietly happy like a little child.

"There, Albert, read that."

Now the red paper can be removed from the lamp, the plate held up to the light bulb. Letters, faint letters can be seen on the plate. They only make two sentences and there are some words they have to guess at, but these two sentences provide the solution to the case.

The plate is replaced in the frame with a sheet of copying paper underneath it. "One-two-three-four-five-six-seven." Studer counts slowly, it sounds like an incantation. Then the frame is covered over again and opened away from the light. The paper is developed, fixed, dipped in alcohol then attached with a thread to the post holding the left-hand shutter of the window. Since the right-hand one is open the paper flutters like a pennant in the wind. It's three o'clock in the morning; there's already a gleam of grey over the hills to the east. The two men collapse onto their beds, exhausted. Soon they're asleep.

The dining room, half past seven in the morning. On the white tablecloths are shallow glass dishes with curls of butter, shining metal bowls full of jam and honey, plates of cheese. There's a smell of coffee and hot milk. Only a few tables are taken, one guest here and a woman there with two brats – the brats are licking the jam off the spoon without bothering about bread. Studer thinks modern children are badly brought up. He's freshly shaved, his short hair is gleaming like the coat of a dapple-grey stallion and his moustache has been so carefully combed that both his upper and lower lips are uncovered. If Ottilia, the Italian waitress, were to come near she would notice that the sergeant, like the late Joachim Krock, is "*profumato*". In order to counter the effects of his lack of sleep, Studer emptied the little bottle of eau de Cologne, which was in his suitcase, over his head. It did sting when it got in his eyes, and on his freshly shaven cheeks, but it certainly woke him up. Today he has to be on the alert; he needs to have all his wits about him. During the night – or, to be more precise, the early morning – did Studer not see the ghost the cook had talked about?

Sitting opposite the sergeant is Albert Guhl.

Strange how the younger generation can't take even just one sleepless night. Albert looks tired and out of sorts. It's only when he looks at his father-in-law that his eyes light up. He admires the older man; he can't understand why Marie's father is still only a sergeant.

Albert Guhl, a simple police officer in Arbon, is young; he knows nothing of the business with the bank that cost Studer his comfortable position as chief inspector with the Bern city police. He's not much more than a snotty-nosed kid; he doesn't know yet that there are crossroads in life: the easy road leads to honour and glory, but the toll you must pay to take that road is called self-respect and a clear conscience. It was a toll Studer had refused to pay – his colleagues at headquarters in Bern say he's as stubborn as a mule. There'll come a time when "Bärtu" will find himself at a crossroads as well, but for the moment he's just full of admiration for the piece of magic by which his father-in-law drew letters out of a blank sheet of paper.

Jacques Gardiny, the banker, enters. His paralysis seems to have improved since the previous day. Supported by his nurse, he manages to get to his table. He walks stiffly, legs splayed, like a stork.

There are yellow curtains drawn over the windows looking east; the light in the room is pleasantly subdued. Albert has had two cups of coffee; he's starting to wake up.

Anni Rechsteiner appears in the doorway, wishing her guests a good morning. She has a white bandage on her right arm. Questions about how she came to hurt herself are gently but firmly turned aside. She stops at the sergeant's table, leaning on her left hand, and asks him if he slept well. Studer nods; he can't speak because his mouth's full. Finally he manages to swallow the stubborn roll. He places his large hand with its wide, flat fingertips on Anni's small hand and whispers, "By midday you'll be free."

He can feel that she's trembling all over; her hand clutches the edge of the table so hard the knuckles turn white. Every eye in the room is on him, but he doesn't care. Let them stare! He's just as well dressed as the rest of them; his grey flannel suit looks good on him, just a little baggy round the upper arms, but he can't help that. A man either has muscles or he hasn't.

Ottilia Buffatto comes in with two huge metal jugs: coffee and milk. She collects all the small jugs from the tables, refills them and puts them out again. Studer's never seen that before, so he asks Anni why she doesn't just give her guests the one helping. People shouldn't leave the table still hungry and thirsty, she says. A good principle, the sergeant agrees, but is it economic?

Anni shrugs her shoulders and continues on her way round the room, a "Good morning" here, a "Good morning" there. A brave woman, a woman who can manage without outside help.

Studer crumples up his serviette and drops it on the table. Seeing Albert fold his up and put it in the ring, he indicates with a wave of the hand that it's not necessary. When he's next to him, he whispers that the post bus goes at eleven thirty. Everything will be over by then.

Nine o'clock. Time to go to the post office. Frau Gloor behind the counter greets him with a friendly nod. She hands the sergeant two telegrams.

To open them he goes to the bench against the church wall, surrounded by the new graves and the old ones that have already turned into flowerbeds. Out of his wallet he takes a piece of paper covered all over with numbers and letters. Albert has to get out his notebook; the sergeant dictates slowly to him, letter by letter, the transcription of the one telegram that's written in Polcod. The telegram from Mannheim is long. Studer dictates quickly, but still a gleam appears in the young officer's eyes. He seems surprised by what it says. Studer himself has to translate the telegram from Paris. Just think: he's got a son-in-law who can't even read French properly. It's enough to make you tear your hair out.

Half past nine. Just time to look in at the bicycle shop. Bruin comes up sadly to say good morning, wags his tail, his eyes full of questions.

"Yes," says the sergeant, "your master'll be home this

evening. Or tomorrow morning at the latest. Good morning, Fräulein Loppacher. I meant to ask: are you thinking of going back to St Gallen?"

Silence. A long silence. Then, hesitantly, "If Ernst wants me, I'll stay here."

"That's sensible," says Studer, adding, with a wide grin, "but it'll ruin your manicure, I'm afraid."

For answer Martha Loppacher wordlessly holds out her hands to him, backs upwards. The nails have been cut short; the polish is flaking off in places. Her cheeks are red, but it's a natural red. What more could a man ask for? Sergeant Studer feels he'd really like to give her a pat on the cheek, as if she were a little child that's been good. Since he can hardly do that, he just says: "That's the ticket. But after all the lies you've dished up, Martheli, it's about time you did me a favour. I want you to be in the hotel at half past ten. Show me your watch."

They compare. Martha Loppacher's watch is five minutes fast.

"Half past ten, then? On the dot. The first-floor corridor, outside room 8, right?" The ex-typist nods.

"What's Fritz doing?"

Fritz is sitting on a pile of blankets in the room beside the workshop, a bottle of milk in his right hand with a what do you call it, a teat on the end. He's giving Ideli the piglet its breakfast. Studer doesn't stay long. There's no reason to torment the poor fellow, who made him welcome in the company of animals and chatted to him during the night in such a good-natured fashion. The sergeant tells him to write him a letter: Sergeant Jakob Studer, 98 Thunstrasse, Bern. Can he remember that? Yes? OK. And he's to give Ernst, the "reg'lar buck", the sergeant's greetings and wish him all the best from him on his marriage.

Ten o'clock. Johannes Küng has mown the meadow behind the hotel. Now he's pulling a two-wheeled cart and loading up the mown grass. The man does a proper job, you have to give him that. Anni won't be left completely on her own once Studer's gone back to Bern. He finds that reassuring.

Four men are coming across the meadow: Dr Schläpfer the examining magistrate, Zuberbühler the chief of Appenzell police, a nameless secretary and an equally nameless detective.

"We have carried out your instructions," says Dr Schläpfer. "To the letter, Herr Studer." (Herr! Whatever next?) "And we've had a report from the Federal Prosecutor's Office. At the last minute the St Gallen chief of police wanted to tag along, but I rang him up to say no thank you. We're better off sorting this out *entre nous* – among ourselves."

"I can understand French, Herr Doctor," Studer says mildly, at which the examining magistrate blushes.

"Yes, I know, Sergeant. The people in Bern can't praise you highly enough. Their only regret is that you keep on causing . . . giving cause for . . . for . . ."

The learned gentleman starts getting tangled up in his own sentence and Studer mercifully interrupts with an "*A bah*! That's neither here nor there. The main thing is to put a stop to their little game."

"But treading carefully, Herr Studer, very carefully. Otherwise there might be diplomatic repress—"

"The people in the capital," says Studer, "seem to be turning into real scared cats. The least threat and they're hi—"

"Shh, Sergeant, shh. Not so loud."

The back door that Studer has used so often. He gives the other four a sign to wait, then slips into the hotel and has a peep into the dining room. Jacques Gardiny is no longer there. He goes back to the door, puts his finger to his lips and sits down on the stairs. Then he takes his shoes off. The four men do likewise and in their stockinged feet they creep up the stairs. None of the floorboards creak, nor do the hinges of the door to room 8, and the group assembles in Studer's room unseen and unheard. Albert, who left his father-in-law when he went to Graf's house, is at the window. He is introduced. "How do you do?" – "Pleased to met you." All in a whisper.

What is this the sergeant's pulling out from under his mattress? To their astonishment the four gentlemen see that it is straw, damp straw.

"An old trick," the sergeant whispers. "I would have liked to use the other one, Dr Eisenbarth's trick, but it wouldn't work here. Twenty-five past ten. I've just time to tell you the story. Some lady, a countess or suchlike, gets taken to Eisenbarth in her sedan chair. She whines on and on at the doctor. She's paralysed, it's been three years now, she's tried everything, nothing's worked, but she knows Dr Eisenbarth will heal her. The doctor – ah, here comes his fellow practitioner. Good morning, Dr Salvisberg, I'm just telling them a story. Eisenbarth hasn't got a proper surgery; he's got a caravan in which he travels round the fairs. He has a look at the woman, picks her up and carries her into his caravan. Then he whispers something to his servant who, after a while, comes back carrying a basket, with a cloth covering it. Now at that period the ladies wore crinolines. Looking her straight in the eye, Eisenbarth tells her to stand up. He has such a compelling stare that the countess suddenly finds herself on her feet in front of him. At a sign from the doctor, the servant slips the basket under the crinoline and whips off the cloth.

Then Eisenbarth gives the countess a push; she stumbles and falls down, right on the basket. But with a scream she's back on her feet again, dancing round the caravan, down the steps, across the market square and all the way home. Dr Eisenbarth is left in the caravan, smiling at the basket, which is full to the brim with nettles – Shh. Shh! Not so loud." The gentlemen stifle their laughter in their handkerchiefs.

Suddenly they fall silent. A voice out in the corridor asks if he can see Herr Rechsteiner. Anni's voice says yes.

"The pastor," Studer whispers. "One minute to go. As I said, it's an old trick. I read about it in a book when I was a lad. A very well-known book."

Quietly Studer creeps out into the corridor. He piles up the damp straw outside a door further down the corridor, comes back and gives his orders. Then he takes out a box of matches and lights one – in his own room, so the noise won't give him away; a piece of newspaper flares up (the four gentlemen are amazed at the sergeant's agility, despite his heavy frame) and Studer shoves the blazing newspaper under the straw. It smoulders, smokes – but the draught is coming from room 8 and blows the smoke in through the gaps in the door without a number, the door to Rechsteiner's bedroom. And now six male voices are shouting, "Fire! Fire!" A click. It's not the door with the smoking straw that opens, however, but a door to the right of it, in a dark passageway.

Rechsteiner is standing in the doorway. He's shoved his nightshirt into a pair of trousers and pulled on a jacket. He stands there, blinking his eyes in the smoke. Behind him is the pastor. The door to room 7 opens too and Herr Gardiny, the banker from Paris, takes a few hesitant steps out into the corridor. Steps come hurrying up the stairs. First Ottilia Buffatto appears, then Fräulein Loppacher, finally Johannes Küng. Studer turns to him and tells him to throw the straw out of the window. Which he does. The smoke disperses. Then Detective Sergeant Studer of the Bern Cantonal Police – speaking formal German, no better and no worse than Martha Loppacher – begs the gentlemen to be so good as to come into the room.

Karl Rechsteiner, landlord of the Hôtel zum Hirschen, goes pale and staggers, but two women support him, Anni on the right and Otti on the left. With their help he manages to get to his bed – his bed which is so conveniently placed: with his left hand he can open the window in the wall beside his bed, and in the summer the balcony door is wide open anyway.

Dr Salvisberg bends over his patient. It's obvious Rechsteiner isn't shamming; his face has a greenish tinge. Without the doctor needing to ask, Studer brings the box with the oil of camphor ampoules and the syringes from the adjoining room, Anni's bedroom. Soon Rechsteiner can breathe easily again. But Dr Salvisberg shakes his head, concerned, then whispers, "He hasn't long to go . . . his heart . . ."

Anni Rechsteiner has heard his words as well. In silence she arranges the pillows for her dying husband, forgetting the wound in her own arm, the wound her husband made the previous day when she woke too soon from her sleep – despite the sleeping draught – and saw him come in and bend over her bed. She managed to ward off the knife, then she screamed and kept on screaming as she leaped out of bed and followed her husband into the adjoining room, flung open the door – and fainted just as Studer was coming to help.

She plumps up the pillows, makes her husband comfortable, pulls up the blankets, goes to get a little bottle from the next room, pours some drops on her handkerchief and moistens the sick man's forehead with some fragrant lavender-water. Then she sits down and takes his hand in hers. Suddenly she looks up, searching, searching. Finally she sees Studer. The look in her eye is one of reproach.

Studer's Revelations

There's not enough space for everyone, so the minor characters are put in Frau Anni's room, the door being left open so everyone can hear. In Rechsteiner's room are: the examining magistrate and the chief of police, Sergeant Studer and his son-in-law, Gardiny, the banker from Paris; Ottilia Buffatto and Martha Loppacher are in Anni's room, beyond the secretary, who has a notebook on his knee. Dr Salvisberg is sitting on the ledge of the open window, to the left of his patient.

Rechsteiner's eyes are wide open; his gaze flickers back and forward between the sergeant and his wife.

"Can you hear me, Rechsteiner?" Studer asked. The sick man nodded. "Shall I go through what happened and you can interrupt and correct me if I get something wrong?" Another nod. So the Bern detective began his account.

"The first thing that struck me about this case was the lengths to which the murderer had gone to divert suspicion onto several people. The spoke pointed to the bicycle-shop owner, but the letters to Martha Loppacher. The first question I asked myself was why just the letters had been taken and not the envelopes as well? The answer was simple: without the empty envelopes no one would have ever had the idea that there had been letters from Martha Loppacher in the dead man's wallet. I asked you, Dr Schläpfer, if I could keep three of the envelopes. You will remember that I spoke my request out loud, when the waitress, the landlady and Johannes Küng were all nearby. Joachim Krock was not far away either. If I kept the three envelopes, the natural thing was for the murderer to assume I had discovered something on them; he would be afraid and that would make him do something stupid.

"He poisoned my vermouth."

Exclamations of surprise. Dr Schläpfer repeated, "Your vermouth?"

"Yes," said Studer impassively. "I swapped my glass with Krock's. And once you have heard the rest of my story, you will have no sympathy with Joachim Krock.

"It was Krock who was meant to drink the *Wormet* anyway, wasn't it, Rechsteiner?"

The sick man nodded, kept on nodding. Then the hand that looked like a crab with a pale calcareous shell was raised and pointed behind them, to the door to the neighbouring room where Ottilia Buffatto, the waitress, was sitting beside the typist Martha Loppacher.

"In the late afternoon," Rechsteiner said, panting and wheezing – it reminded Studer of a dredger they use to clear out harbours and rivers, the huge buckets bringing up all sorts of things: sand, rubbish and, occasionally, shells which look drab on the outside but shimmer with all the colours of the rainbow on the inside: mother of pearl. "In the late afternoon Anni" (he spoke his wife's name carefully, tenderly) "always has a lie-down. So I got up and took out the box of pills. In here," he said, opening the drawer of his bedside table, "I have a spirit stove. And here an iron spoon. And there're plenty of empty bottles —" He tried to laugh, but all that came out was a croak that turned into a thick cough. "I filled the spoon with water, heated it, put the pills in one after the other and emptied the solution into an empty medicine bottle. Then I slipped out – through Anni's room. 'Fetch the vermouth,' I told Otti, asking her which was Krock's place. She showed me, I poured the contents of the medicine bottle into the glass and Otti filled it up with vermouth. But the girl tricked me. Tricked me, Studer! It wasn't meant for you, not for you at all, but for that swine Krock."

Exhausted, he fell silent.

"I know, Rechsteiner," said Studer. "You wanted to put things right. But the others didn't."

"How . . . how do you know that, Studer?"

The sergeant took a photograph out of his pocket. It looked like an ancient document, faded from exposure to the sun and the wind, to the rain as well, but with an effort the words could still be made out. Some letters were missing, but the meaning was clear.

".hat .echst.iner ..tends to de..roy all t.e IO.s he's .ot p.op. e to sig. a.. to t..t end .e is go..g t. cont... t.e a.tho.it.es."

"That Rechsteiner intends to destroy all the IOUs he's got people to sign and to that end he is going to contact the authorities."

Studer read it out and asked if that was correct, directing his question at the other room.

Martha Loppacher nodded. She'd written that last Tuesday. But there was a world of difference between Tuesday and Saturday.

"A world of difference!" Studer smiled. "The world of difference came from the fact that in that time Martha here and Ernst Graf, the 'reg'lar buck'," – Studer tried to imitate the Appenzell dialect and failed so miserably they all laughed, despite the presence of a man on his deathbed, who for his part joined in the laughter – "had fallen in love," he concluded when the laughter had died down.

"To understand all this, we have to go back to the beginning," he said, leaning his elbows on his spread thighs and clasping his hands. He seemed to find his thumbnails particularly interesting and did not raise his eyes from them.

"Over ten years ago, when peace finally arrives after four years of war, a man leaves home. He goes to Germany. In Switzerland he's worked in hotels, first of all as a bellboy, then on room service and finally he was allowed to serve in the restaurant. He goes to Germany because he believes, quite rightly believes, the starved country, partly occupied by foreign troops, will want to make up for the years of deprivation during the war. He doesn't go to Berlin, but to Mannheim. The Palatinate is occupied, including Ludwigshafen; the foreign officers will probably come across the bridge to Mannheim on the other side of the Rhine. He gets a position as *maître d'hôtel* at the Kaiserhof Hotel. There he encounters the post-war world: bankers – German, French, American. He becomes particularly friendly with a French banker – as far as one can talk of friendship between a power in the world of high finance and a waiter, even a head waiter. Rechsteiner's clever, adroit. He manages to bring the French banker and the burgomaster of the city together; how doesn't concern us here. A large-scale fraud involving illegal currency transfers comes off. Rechsteiner has been useful, but the French banker is not a man to put himself at the mercy of a subordinate without taking precautions. A shady piece of business is set up (in those times there was no problem finding accomplices for that kind of thing); Rechsteiner is accused of having forged a cheque for 50,000 marks and is arrested. The Frenchman bribes the prison guard (remember there was a revolution going on in Germany at the time), Rechsteiner escapes and returns to Switzerland. In Zurich he meets the Frenchman again, who tells him what the situation is: the trial has taken place in Mannheim, Rechsteiner has been sentenced to ten years in prison, at any moment the German government can demand his extradition. But he will be safe, as long as he goes along with the Frenchman's arrangements – of course, the moment he steps out of line, a letter will be sent to police headquarters in Mannheim, his extradition will be requested . . . But that is not what the Frenchman wants. On the contrary. There's ten thousand francs; Rechsteiner can use it to buy himself a hotel; later on, well, they'll just have to see . . . There are also papers in the name of Rechsteiner – the name of the man we can see here in bed is different, he's taken his mother's name. Rechsteiner's happy with that. He goes to St Gallen, meets the housekeeper of a hotel, falls in love with her. They decide to get married and set up on their own: the Hôtel zum Hirschen in Schwarzenstein is bought. They live happily – but not ever after. Rechsteiner has forgotten his problems in Germany, but five years later he's reminded of them.

"Slowly the embroidery crisis begins to make itself felt in Appenzell. Then one day, out of the blue, Rechsteiner receives a letter from St Gallen with the Frenchman's signature: he is to follow the instructions of Krock's Information Bureau in every detail.

"The instructions are not long in coming. Rechsteiner's to be the go-between. He's to persuade all his neighbours to borrow money from him. He's well liked in the area, everyone trusts him, he manages to get them to sign the IOUs and the interest he collects each year goes to the office in St Gallen.

"The French banker hasn't changed his methods very much. Just as, immediately after the war, he had systematically sucked dry a country whose confidence had been sapped by war, revolution and occupation, so now he has been 'investing' capital in a canton where people have been demoralized by unemployment. He waits, two years, three years, then calls in his loans as a way of acquiring land cheaply. What he intends to do with all the land I don't know, that's none of my business.

"I called the man behind Krock's Information Bureau, the man who has been using it to tyrannize Rechsteiner, a Frenchman. That is not true. As far as I know – and my knowledge comes from a reliable source: I have a good friend who holds a senior post in the *Police judiciaire* – the man is no more French than the other large-scale swindlers who are feeding off France like maggots in a juicy joint of meat. But on paper he's French – isn't that so, Herr Gardiny?"

The thrust was so unexpected that everyone in the room started. Only the banker sat there, unmoved and unmoving. After a moment he placed a gloved hand over his mouth, to conceal a yawn.

"Rechsteiner falls ill," Studer went on. "Since a sick man can't be trusted, they place someone in the house to keep him under constant observation . . . Didn't they, Otti?"

"To you I'm not Otti, I'm Fräulein Buffatto," came the indignant reply from the other room. Laughter, suppressed laughter. Studer continued:

"Rechsteiner's genuinely ill, he has consumption. According to the doctor he has three or four years to live. In order to at least be able to die in peace, he had a brilliant idea: he won't get up any more; he'll say he's paralysed. Dr Salvisberg, who has been treating him, will back me up that in Rechsteiner's present condition paralysis is very difficult to determine. And then —"

"—a horizontal posture is clearly indicated for a patient in the later stages of tuberculosis," the doctor broke in, "perfectly appropriate."

"As I was going to say. However, Rechsteiner did not invest Herr Gardiny's capital in Schwarzenstein alone but in the neighbouring villages as well. Fräulein Buffatto (the emphasis on the last two words brought a flush to Studer's face) took over the task of maintaining contact between creditors and debtors."

Silence. A murky silence, filling the room with its waves and eddies. Someone cleared their throat impatiently; the secretary coughed. Herr Gardiny, the banker from Paris, took a gold case out of his pocket, extracted a cigarette and lit it with a lighter. Sergeant Studer stood up, snatched the cigarette from Gardiny's lips, threw it out of the window, sat down again and said, in a matter-of-fact voice: "Smoking makes you cough, doesn't it, Rechsteiner?" The sick man nodded vigorously, a shy smile appearing at the corners of his mouth. He took his wife's hand and laid his head on it.

"I've almost finished," Studer said. "Fräulein Buffatto writes to St Gallen. There they decide – as is done with suspect civilians during war – to billet someone in the hotel. Jean Stieger volunteers. One last digression: like all scoundrels, this scum, Krock, Stieger and Gardiny, don't trust anybody, so the Information Bureau took on the brother of the bicycle-shop owner as messenger boy. Ernst Graf lives next door to Rechsteiner and they hoped his brother would provide additional surveillance of the hotel. In that they weren't entirely successful.

"Jean Stieger arrives. Fräulein Ottilia Buffatto has managed to turn Rechsteiner so far against his wife that he has handed over control of the accounts to her. But Frau Rechsteiner needs money. A cow died three months ago and needs to be replaced; Anni wants to save her husband worry, so she buys another cow – but that means two thousand francs are missing. She still has some savings, but they are invested in shares in a mountain railway. The price is low at the moment, but her husband has spoken so often of Krock's firm in St Gallen, she's seen the address so often that, all unknowing, she turns to them."

Anni Rechsteiner stared at her old childhood sweetheart, wide-eyed. How did the man know all this? Studer gave her a friendly smile and continued:

"Jean Stieger brings the money. But he refuses to hand it over until Anni gives her waitress the day off. Why? I don't think we need to go into that. But what the idiot doesn't know is that the waitress is working for the same side as he is. He's just a young puppy who got taken on because he had connections. Frau Rechsteiner refuses.

It's her money the lad has and he has no right to make conditions.

"She gets worked up and goes to tell her husband a representative from Krock's Bureau has arrived. Hardly has she left than Otti – sorry, Fräulein Buffatto appears, she too complaining bitterly about the young puppy.

"Then Rechsteiner's alone again. He's probably been thinking: it's bad enough being under the Frenchman's thumb, but to be harassed by some nasty young whipper-snapper, that's really too much. As well as that, Rechsteiner's got a guilty conscience. Hasn't he already started to collect up the IOUs? He can't do it himself. He has to be careful. He sent Martha Loppacher round to the local farmers on Friday and she came back with the news that Krock had already started demanding repayment.

"The corridor's empty. It's half past nine. I'd already told Rechsteiner we'd be going back in the carriages at half past ten. He thinks he has enough time. Every day since he pretended to be paralysed he's got up and walked round the room; sometimes during the night when his wife was asleep, exhausted, he went down as far as the kitchen, or up to the attic, so he's had plenty of practice. He slips out of the back door. What weapon can he use? He sees a rusty spoke from a bicycle wheel in the grass. Küng's busy in the stables; beside the stables is the workshop and there's a vice in there. Five minutes and the spoke has a sharp point. A further five minutes and the handle's ready: he cuts a thread in the blunt end of the spoke, then all he needs to do is to bore a hole in the piece of wood he's using as a handle and the thread will grip. Rechsteiner lies in wait, trembling with cold and fear and anticipation. At twenty to ten Jean Stieger comes out of the back door (probably looking for the waitress) and Rechsteiner waves him over. The two have never met, but Rechsteiner's had two descriptions of him and that's sufficient. He introduces himself and, under the pretence that he has something important to tell him, lures the young man into the garden. Then —"

"Ssstoppit, Sstuuuder, ssstoppit! Pleeease ssstop . . ."

The whimpering from the bed was unbearable.

"I've finished," said the sergeant. "Oh, one more thing. Where's the pastor?"

A deep voice came from Anni's bedroom. "Here."

"You've got the stuff?" said Studer, falling into dialect.

"What d'you think, Sergeant? Course I have."

It was only with reluctance that "Fräulein" Buffatto made way for him. She gave Gardiny a sharp glance, but the banker did not respond, so the waitress had to look on as the bundle of IOUs was handed over to the sergeant. He quickly counted them – thirty – and passed them on to the examining magistrate.

"That is my property," Gardiny said, in soft, impassive tones.

"Is that so?" said Dr Schläpfer. "But the IOUs are all made in the name of Rechsteiner. Do you relinquish all claim to these, Rechsteiner?"

"I do – gladly."

"Put them in the Krock file," said Dr Schläpfer, handing the bundle to his secretary.

Studer opened the door. Slowly the gathering filed out of the room. The sergeant heard Zuberbühler, the chief of police, whisper to Dr Salvisberg, "Can he be moved?"

"Out of the question," the doctor snapped. Despite the fact that Rechsteiner had been wandering round the house for the last three days like an unquiet spirit, he went on, it was all over with him. As his doctor he would not take responsibility for his being moved. The chief of police looked at the examining magistrate, who shook his head. But then he made a sign to the policemen, who nodded and pushed his way out after Ottilia. "Take Buffatto along with you," he said outside.

Downstairs Zuberbühler blew long and loud on his police whistle. The police cars drew up. "Room for me and my son-in-law?" Studer asked. Of course there was. Dr Schläpfer, examining magistrate in Appenzell, could not begin to say how pleased he was. "Of course you'll have dinner with us in Heiden this evening," he insisted as the car set off. Studer shook his head. He yawned. He'd be quite happy if they could drop him off in Arbon, he said, he just wanted to sleep, sleep, sleep.

And get back to Bern that evening.

And that's what happened.

One lunchtime – several weeks had passed since the events in Schwarzenstein – Studer found a letter on his plate. The address was a masterpiece of calligraphy, the letter no less. It said:

Dear Sergeant Studer,

With the present letter I take the liberty of presuming on your time with some good news. (Studer frowned and muttered, "*Chabis!*") Your esteemed intervention has resulted in the release of my brother Ernst from both prison and the threat of prosecution. He is now in the best of health and back in his workshop in Schwarzenstein, whither Fräulein (as was) Martha Loppacher has accompanied him as his spouse. May God grant them every joy and a long and happy married life. His animals too are delighted to see him in such excellent health, which I can say for myself as well. Bruin the dog does sometimes seem to wonder where Sergeant Studer is.

As for myself, I have managed to find employment in the Hôtel zum Hirschen, in which establishment I am occupied in kitchen and cellar, in stable and garden, in the fields and woods. After the death of her dearly beloved husband, Frau Anni Rechsteiner-Ibach was very lonely, but was greatly comforted by the kind attention of our pastor. Hoping that this letter finds you and your good lady in the best of health, I remain,

Your obedient servant,

Fritz Graf

"*Merci*, Hedy," said Sergeant Studer as his wife filled his bowl with soup. "You know," he said after stirring his soup for a while, "if I didn't have you I could be a hotel owner by now."

Frau Studer sighed, but it didn't sound like a genuine sigh and when the sergeant looked up, he saw his wife was smiling.

"What are you laughing at?"

"Oh, Köbu, just thank the Lord you don't own a hotel."

Studer wanted to know why he should thank the Lord.

The answer came back immediately: because he'd spend all day playing billiards and drink too much vermouth.

FEVER

Friedrich Glauser

"With good reason, the German language prize for detective fiction is named after Glauser. . . He has Simenon's ability to turn a stereotype into a person, and the moral complexity to appeal to justice over the head of police procedure."
Times Literary Supplement

When two women are "accidentally" killed by gas leaks, Sergeant Studer investigates the thinly disguised double murder in Bern and Basel. The trail leads to a geologist dead from a tropical fever in a Moroccan Foreign Legion post and a murky oil deal involving rapacious politicians and their henchmen. With the help of a hashish-induced dream and the common sense of his stay-at-home wife, Studer solves the multiple riddles on offer. But assigning guilt remains an elusive affair.

Fever, a European crime classic, was first published in 1936 and is the third in the Sergeant Studer series published by Bitter Lemon Press.

Praise for Glauser's other Sergeant Studer novels

"*Thumbprint* is a fine example of the craft of detective writing in a period which fans will regard as the golden age of crime fiction." *Sunday Telegraph*

"*Thumbprint* is a genuine curiosity that compares to the dank poetry of Simenon and reveals the enormous debt owed by Dürenmatt, Switzerland's most famous crime writer, for whom this should be seen as a template." *Guardian*

"A despairing plot about the reality of madness and life, leavened at regular intervals with strong doses of bittersweet irony. The idiosyncratic investigation of *In Matto's Realm* and its laconic detective have not aged one iota." *Guardian*

"Glauser was among the best European crime writers of the inter-war years. The detail, place and sinister characters are so intelligently sculpted that the sense of foreboding is palpable." *Glasgow Herald*

£9.99/$14.95
Crime paperback original
ISBN 1–904738–14–1/978–1904738–14–5
www.bitterlemonpress.com

FRAMED

Tonino Benacquista

"One of France's leading crime and mystery authors."
Guardian

Antoine's life is good. During the day he hangs pictures for the most fashionable art galleries in Paris. Evenings he dedicates to the silky moves and subtle tactics of billiards, his true passion. But when Antoine is attacked by an art thief in a gallery his world begins to fall apart. His maverick investigation triggers two murders – he finds himself the prime suspect for one of them – as he uncovers a cesspool of art fraud. A game of billiards decides the outcome of this violently funny tale, laced with brilliant riffs about the world of modern art and the parasites that infest it.

In 2004 Bitter Lemon Press introduced Tonino Benacquista to English-speaking readers with the critically acclaimed novel *Holy Smoke*.

PRAISE FOR *FRAMED*

"Screenwriter for the award-winning French crime movie
***The Beat That My Heart Skipped*, Tonino Benacquista is also**
a wonderful observer of everyday life, petty evil and the
ordinariness of crime. The pace never falters as personal
grief collides with outrageous humour and a biting running
commentary on the crooked world of modern art."
Guardian

"Edgy, offbeat black comedy." *The Times*

"Flip and frantic foray into art galleries and billiards halls of
modern Paris." *Evening Standard*

"A black comedy that is set in Paris but reflects its author's
boisterous Italian sensibility. The manic tale is told by an
apprentice picture-hanger who encounters a thief in a
fashionable art gallery and becomes so caught up in a case of
art fraud that he himself 'touches up' a Kandinsky."
New York Times

£9.99/$14.95
Crime paperback original
ISBN 1–904738–16–8/978–1904738–16–9
www.bitterlemonpress.com

HAVANA BLACK

Leonardo Padura

A MARIO CONDE MYSTERY

"The mission of that enterprising Bitter Lemon Press is to publish English translations of the best foreign crime fiction. The newest addition to its list is the prize-winning Cuban novelist Leonardo Padura" *The Telegraph*

The brutally mutilated body of Miguel Forcade is discovered washed up on a Havana beach. Head smashed in by a baseball bat, genitals cut off with a blunt knife. Forcade was once responsible for confiscating art works from the bourgeoisie fleeing the revolution. Had he really returned from exile just to visit his ailing father?

Lieutenant Mario Conde immerses himself in Cuba's dark history, expropriations of priceless paintings now vanished without trace, corruption and old families who appear to have lost much, but not everything.

Padura evokes the disillusionment of a generation, yet this novel is a eulogy to Cuba, and to the great friendships of those who chose to stay and fight for survival.

PRAISE FOR *HAVANA BLACK*

"A great plot, perfectly executed with huge atmosphere. You can almost smell the cigar smoke, rum and cheap women." *Daily Mirror*

"This is a strong tasting book. A rich feast of wit and feeling." *The Independent*

"Well-plotted second volume of Padura's seething, steamy Havana Quartet. This densely packed mystery should attract readers outside the genre." *Publishers Weekly*

"Lt. Mario Conde, known on the street as 'the Count,' is prone to metaphysical reflection on the history of his melancholy land but the city of Havana keeps bursting through his meditations, looking very much alive." *New York Times*

£9.99/$14.95
Crime paperback original
ISBN 1–904738–15–X/978–1904738–15–2
www.bitterlemonpress.com

THE MANNEQUIN MAN

Luca Di Fulvio

Shortlisted for the European Crime Writing Prize

"Di Fulvio exposes souls with the skills of a surgeon, It's like turning the pages of something forbidden – seduction, elegant and dangerous." *Alan Rickman*

"Know why she's smiling?" he asked, pointing a small torch at the corpse. "Fish hooks. Two fish hooks at the corners of her mouth, a bit of nylon, pull it round the back of the head and tie a knot. Pretty straightforward, right?" Amaldi noticed the metallic glint at the corners of the taut mouth.

Inspector Amaldi has enough problems. A city choked by a pestilent rubbish strike, a beautiful student harassed by a telephone stalker, a colleague dying of cancer and the mysterious disappearance of arson files concerning the city's orphanage. Then the bodies begin to appear.

This novel of violence and decay, with its vividly portrayed characters, takes place over a few oppressive weeks in an unnamed Italian city that strongly evokes Genoa.

The Italian press refers to Di Fulvio as a grittier, Italian Thomas Harris, and *Eyes of Crystal*, the film of the novel, was launched at the 2004 Venice Film Festival.

" A novel that caresses and kisses in order to violate the reader with greater ease." *Rolling Stone*

"A powerful psycho-thriller of spine-shivering intensity . . . written with immense intelligence and passionate menace. Not to be read alone at night." *The Times*

"A wonderful first novel that will seduce the fans of deranged murderers in the style of Hannibal Lecter. And beautifully written to boot." *RTL*

£9.99/$14.95
Crime paperback original
ISBN 1–904738–13–3/978–1904738–13–8
www.bitterlemonpress.com